D0910938

PRECIOUS TREASURES
From GRANDIE RIVER

WILTON BROOMES

BookVenture Publishing LLC
1000 Country Lane Ste 300
Ishpeming MI 49849
www.bookventure.com
Hotline: 1(877) 276-9751
Fax: 1(877) 864-1686

Ordering Information:
Quantity sales. Special discounts are available on quantity purchases by corporations, associations, and others. For details, contact the publisher at the address above.

Printed in the United States of America.

Library of Congress Control Number	2018958398
ISBN-13:	
Softcover	978-1-64166-988-7
Pdf	978-1-64166-989-4
ePub	978-1-64166-990-0
Kindle	978-1-64166-991-7

Rev. date: 11/05/2018

CONTENTS

DEDICATION

I WISH TO DEDICATE THIS book to Mrs. English and Miss Posio who were instructors in a *Short Story Writing* course at Voorhee's Campus, New York City Community College many years ago, and whose course I took as a departmental elective. I often looked back at those sessions as being some of the most delightful of all my college classes. I would reminisce at how at times the American students, all of whom were much younger than a group of foreign students; and, they and our instructors seemed to be confused by the non-American clique, and couldn't seem to remember from which country each of them had come; I was a part of that foreign clique. We amused ourselves by their confusion and we deliberately tried to keep them guessing.

There were Joseph Bell from Guyana, Glenn Townsend from Jamaica, Guillaume Marcel from Haiti, Charles Marfo from Ghana, Felex Arogundarde from Nigeria, Peter George from Trinidad, and yours truly from Tobago. After we graduated from that college some us went on to higher education elsewhere, while others returned to their homelands; but, we didn't keep in touch with each other, and I often wondered what has become of all of them. If any of them recognize me from this book, please, let us get in touch with each other.

ATTENTION

Please see KEY at the end of this book for interpretation of some passages of this book where the local dialect is used.

PREFACE

I WAS IN A STORE in Newark, New Jersey, when I overheard a conversation between two women:

First woman said, "Ah finish shoppin', oui" Her companion said, "Yuh get al yuh want?" The first woman replied, "Yes, man."

I walked over and asked, "Trinis?"

The first woman looked at me, pointed to her companion and said, "She is."

I said, "And which island are you from?"

She said that she was from Germany, but that she was living in Trinidad for the past two years.

I said, "And you picked up that Trinidad accent so fast?"

She said, "Thank yuh; well, ah ha tuh duh, wha' ah ha tuh duh."

In her first remark she used the word "oui" which is a French word that means "yes" or "indeed". Trinidad was once settled by France, and the unique Trinidad vernacular is derived from a mixture of the languages spoken by the various peoples that inhabited the island in the past. This is not to be unexpected, for even in the English language one could find words from other languages, which were borrowed by the British, and have become part of the English language.

That German woman was speaking like a real Trinidadian. She even threw in some interjections as "ewee" and "arm, arm" in her sentences; just as a born Trinidadian would do. These are expressions that a Trinidadian would use when pausing in her speech, and searching for some way to express herself. You will note also, that in her reply to her friend the woman had said, "Yes, man," even though she was speaking to a woman. A Trinidadian would address someone as "man" or "George" in a similar manner as an American would address someone as "Joe", even though that's not his name.

In the 1960s and 1970s it was very difficult for some West Indians to be understood when speaking to the average American; whereas, the average West Indian could understand most Americans because they were exposed to the various American accents through radio, television, and the movies. Therefore, of necessity, the West Indian would try to speak like an American. However, as more and more West Indians came to America, and as the American ear had become more attuned to the West Indian speech, the West Indian began to feel more comfortable speaking the way he does.

I had met a gentleman whom I thought was Jamaican, and evening after evening, we would talk to each other in a Caribbean dialect, until one evening when he was with some American friends, and he had called me over to converse; the group were all smiling at each other every time I turned away, even though this fellow was also speaking as a West Indian. I got to find out that he was not West Indian at all; his parents were; but, he was born and grew up in America. A Jamaican dialect was spoken at home, but he normally spoke as an American elsewhere. From state to state in America there may be a variation of the American accent; even from one community to another. Therefore, to speak with an accent, is nothing to be ashamed of in America. I was working with a group of workers and I could tell from just about anywhere someone had come; but there was this one woman who was an exception. One evening I asked her from where she had come, and she said, "Newark, New Jersey." We all had a good laugh because we were working in Newark!

Some parents would forbid their children to speak in their parents' dialect, because they think that it would hinder a child from speaking like an American; but, that's not true: a child is able to handle both languages at the same time. I knew of a Spanish woman who would carry her six-year child with her to act as an interpreter when the woman wanted to transact some business in English. The child had learnt naturally Spanish at home, while he spoke English at school and when he was with some of his friends. In certain southern states in America one could find people who speak just like West Indians do, because their ancestors had come from the Caribbean during the colonial days. Also, I met someone from the Republic of Liberia who was speaking like an American from one of the southern states of America. The company I was working for in America had a subsidiary in Liberia, and he was sent to America at the parent company to see how various operations were performed. As he and I were talking, he reminded me that Liberia was formed in the early 1800s by freed American slaves.

I am writing this preface because some of the conversations in this book were written in a Trinidad and Tobago dialect; However, I'm providing a key for anyone who's unable to understand what is being said. The key is indexed, where applicable, consecutively by chapters. And any remark in the Trinidad and Tobago dialect which needs to be interpreted is written in script, and the interpretation follows in italics.

INTRODUCTION

THIS BOOK IS A literary fiction whose setting began on the Caribbean island of Tobago, but was expanded to Europe and other parts of the world, to mimic the movements of the Caribbean peoples during the Colonial era and after the islands had gained their independence. The book contains elements of some real events, which might have been exaggerated, and were stitched together like the various pieces of fabrics in a quilted sheet in order to link together the discourse of the book.

Where a portion of the book is similar to a real episode, the names of the characters have been changed, and the spellings of some of the characters and places in some conversations were intentionally misspelled in order to imitate the broken English that is commonly spoken in Trinidad and Tobago. The reader is advised not to try to associate any of the names of those characters and places to any real person or location they know, seeing that some of the real stories might not have been connected to each other, or might have been fictitious altogether and just to suite the narrative of this book. The work attempted to capture what life was like during the period which the book covers, and to promote national unity and racial harmony.

CHAPTER ONE

History Classes

M ICKEY LOVED HIS NEW school and especially his history classes. There were two cupboards at the back of his class-room that were full of new books that the government had recently purchased for the school, and because Mickey's teacher quickly discovered that he was an avaricious reader, and not wanting to discourage him, she assigned Mickey to be in charged of all the books. In his spare time he would find himself immersed in reading or putting away books that the other pupils had turned in. It wasn't long before he could tell if any book was missing and where each book should be located.

Some history books about buccaneers, Caribs, Arawaks, and European navigators, who were arriving in the West Indies, were his favorites. Almost every day Mickey would accompany his father in search of feed for their animals from the area around a nearby bay before going to school, and he would pass by Grandie River -- It was more like a swamp; I don't know why it was named a river. A large portion of the swamp was covered with coconut shells, which were f loating on the water, and forming a canopy at that section of the swamp. Away from the banks in the distance, were some mangrove trees looking as an island, or so it seemed, and almost in the middle of Grandie River. The water was very murky and no one knew what was below the canopy. There were stories a long time ago about the sighting of alligators in the area; however, none in recent memory, and when the tide was high, the sea would wash up sand which blocked the swamp from draining into the sea. Also, there was a constant stream of water which was coming from Par Gully, and another tributary named

Horse River, which also flowed into the swamp. The government would send a crew of men from time to time to dig a channel in the sand which was obstructing the f low of the swamp water from draining into the sea.

One morning as Mickey was passing by the swamp alone, he wanted to relieve himself, and went beyond the beach for some privacy beneath some coconut trees in the sandy soil near the swamp where he was digging a hole, which he had intended to cover up afterward. While he was about to relieve himself he remembered the stories he had read in his history books, so he began to look for any human bones that might be buried beneath the sand: the Caribs were said to be cannibals who feasted upon their victims raw -- most often the victims were captured Arawaks. Not very deep in the ground Mickey found evidence of what he hoping to find: a big bone buried not very deep from the surface. Mickey looked for, and found, more bones. He became convinced that he was on the site of a former Carib settlement.

As he surveyed the area: the bay was well protected by Edmond Island, a huge rocky island projecting out of the sea, and which was guarding one's entry into the bay; the area with the mangrove trees in the middle of the swamp was very suitable to conceal any treasures the Caribs might have wanted to hide from the Buccaneers; and the surrounding properties were f lat and looked ideal for a Carib settlement. A few yards in the water and away from the banks of the swamp there was a raft that some boys had made out of buffalo wood. Mickey thought to himself: *If I could make a smaller raft out of bamboo which was washed up on the seashore, I could get to the bigger wooden raft on the swamp.* He did, and before long he was making his way to the mangrove trees in the middle of the swamp. He kept sounding the bottom of the swamp with a long bamboo pole as he drew closer and closer to the mangrove trees and, as the water got shallower and shallower ….. *Thump! Thump!* He struck some things hallow beneath the water. *Hidden treasures!* he thought. A few feet away he struck another object, and another! His first impulse was to investigate further for himself and ascertain what those objects were, but he was afraid of being alone for very long on the swamp.

He decided to return to Grandie River with one of his friends from school; but, *which one of them he could trust?* He couldn't think of any one of them that would keep his discovery a secret. He thought of his dad, but his father had warned him several times before about the dangers of entering the swamp alone and perhaps he might punish Mickey for disobeying his father's command. On the way home he had mixed feelings, *he couldn't tell any of his friends and his father might give him a whipping, but news of his discovery was too much for him to keep as a secret.* Finally, he made up his mind: *no amount of whipping from his dad could be greater than the reward of recovering some sunken treasures; but, how break the news to his father?* He began to tell his dad about his history classes at school -- all the stories he had read about Caribs, Arawaks and buccaneers: the Caribs and Arawaks were original Indians who had inhabited the islands, while the buccaneers were European pirates that robbed passing ships from the Caribbean colonies.

"Imagine, we are walking in the very bays that those people walked. Some of their treasures could be buried right beneath us," he said to his father one morning.

Another day as they were passing the swamp, he asked his dad, "If you had some treasures to hide in this area, where would you put them?" He pointed to the mangrove trees, and said, "I couldn't think of a better place than below those trees away from the banks and in the middle of the swamp."

Yet another day he told his dad about a dream which had a few nights ago: *He had unearthed some big bones which seemed to be like human's at a certain place near to swamp, and as he was looking around the area, he saw the raft on the swamp and ferried himself out to the mangrove trees where he felt some objects which could be chests full of treasures.*

"Your history classes are beginning to keep you awake at nights, I see; if there were any treasures in this area, boy, someone would have found them a long time ago," his dad said to him. Nevertheless, his dad was proud of his son and the boy's keen interest in his history classes. His dad couldn't seem to get him to stop talking about sunken treasures. "Any treasures that a person found, would be considered national artifacts and would belong to the Government," his dad told him. He also told Mickey about a Black man named Mr. Conrod who was working on a piece of ground near a certain bay, and had stumbled upon a buried chest of gold. He reported it to a White landowner who owned the property and took charge of the chest of gold, saying he had to turn it into the Government.

When they had come to the place where Mickey had unearthed the bones a few days before, Mickey ran to the spot. "Look, dad; these are the bones that I had seen in my dream!" His father listened as Mickey told him the dream again. Mickey's dream seemed so believable that his dad was convinced that the boy was onto something; indeed. They took the raft and sailed out to the island of mangrove trees. Mickey pointed to the place he had felt the sunken objects and, sure enough, they felt some things unusual. His dad asked the boy, " Ah who ya already tell bout al dis?" After Mickey had told him no one, he said, "Doe mention ah word bout dis tuh anywane."

That day Mickey went to school as usual, while his dad returned to the swamp with Timothy, Mickey's uncle. They brought along some ropes and grappling hooks which they had made out of old iron pipes. They took turns diving into the swamp to where the sunken objects were, and altogether they recovered four sunken chests. They brought the chests to a bank of the swamp and broke them open.

"Gold, gold!" Uncle Timothy exclaimed, "Weh rich!"

"Ahwee hav tuh protect dese treasures fore deh government tek dem way fram ahwee", said Mickey's father.

Uncle Timothy returned to their homes and saddled two donkeys, while his brother remained to guard the treasures. They were going to transport them to, and conceal the gold in, a cave at Engine Town about five miles away until they could decide what to do about them. The cave was very secluded, and in a nearby ravine below, a little stream was f lowing. There was a very deep hole not far from the ravine and into which about half of the stream would f low whenever it rained heavily in the area. The local people used to call that hole by a vulgar name, Devil Bambam Hole, because it seemed to have no bottom. A huge tree might have occupied the spot once, and when the tree had died, its roots rotted and left the huge hole through which water would enter and tunnel itself underground until it make an exit some two miles away.

The night following the relocation of the gold, it began to rain torrentially and it rained constantly for about a week. Never had they seen so much rain in the Village of Belle Garden. There was a huge deluge in all the creeks, and also, several mud slides in the village. The area around the cave was washed away and water flowed into the cave as far as to where the chests of gold were hidden. So strong was the current of water that it transported the treasures along with uprooted trees and mudslides from avalanches. The stream washed the gold into Devil Bambam Hole and subsequently along to the underground tunnel. The brothers feared that their treasures would be lost, but didn't dare to go out in the storm to move them. Uncle Timothy came over to his brother's house, and he and his brother were so deeply engaged in discussing what they should do, that they didn't hear when Mickey joined them.

"The Buccaneers wold kill wone of deh pirates and leav em tuh guard eny treasurs dey bih ah leav behind," said Mickey. "Meh believe dat deh dead pirate guardin deh treasurs beh angry dat yuh mov dem."

"Nonsense!" said his father.

"Maybe, deh boy right; ena al mi forty-five years ah never cee rain lik dis," said Uncle Timothy.

"Ah wonder how much damag dis rain alredy cause; howeber, ahwee ha tuh wait until dis bad weatha ober, fuh wi tuh fine out."

They waited until the rain had subsided, but couldn't get to the treasures immediately due to mud slides and several fallen trees across the road. Mickey didn't go to school for several days after it had stopped raining because classes had been cancelled. When they were able to venture out, the two men donned long rubber boots and went to see about their treasures. To their dismay the cave had been washed away; however, they felt that there was a possibility that the treasures were buried beneath the debris. They entered the ravine and followed it all the way to where it emptied in Edmond River. A huge mandarin tree had fallen and blocked the exit of a cave which was coming from underground. After they had made a thorough search of the area, they returned home very dejected.

While they were gone Mickey had ventured out to a ridge beyond their house to view Edmond River which was about half a mile away in a valley below, and was passing through a coconut estate. Among the debris from the river that was empting into Edmond Bay, Mickey thought he could see what appeared to be a person with rubber boots f loating at the top of water in the river. He called out to his mom Nellie and siblings Donna and Selwyn. "Maybe Dad and Uncle Timothy get catch up inah deh riber and ah beh wash out tuh sea," he said. As he was pointing to what he believed was a person f loating in the river, his mother assured him that the men were experienced, and knew how to be careful. Though they were concerned about their dad and uncle, the children were gazing at the various patterns that the debris from the river was making upon the ocean as the river was pushing the debris out to sea. When his dad and uncle returned, the children were still viewing the river and the sea, which was then covered with mud and trees, as far as eyes could see.

"Ahwee beh think dat deh riber beh haul ahyoh way," Mickey said to them.

"Eh didn't," his dad replied, "but eh seem as though ahwee lost deh chest ah gold."

Very tired and dejected, the men washed themselves and turned in for that day, but they had resolved to continue their search for the treasures at some other time. In the meanwhile, one day Mr. Stanley Willis who used to set fish traps all along the river had gone to repair his traps: he would make fences out of bamboo trunks and coconut branches in several places across the entire width of the river. The river would continue to flow through the coconut branches, but a fish could not pass the barrier. However, he would place fish traps through the branches. The traps were cones made out of bamboo. A fish would enter the open end of a trap, and get caught in the narrow end of a cone. He had several of those fences, and cones at various locations. One day as he was at a certain place where there was a gravel bed beside the river, he saw one of the chests which had washed upon the gravel bed; but, as he was approaching it, he noticed an alligator sunning itself not very far away. He was getting ready to shoot the alligator, when it crawled into the river and disappeared beneath the water. He approached the chest, and when he had broken it open, he saw that it was full of gold.

Mr. Stanley Willis was a watchman for the estate through which the river ran. It was said that he couldn't read nor write, and that he mistrusted commercial banks, and would have the White man, Mr. Peter Scott, for whom he was working, keep all his pay. Besides giving him a weekly allowance, Mr. Scott would buy him such things as he needed from town for his family whenever the boss drove into town on weekends. On the day in which he found the chest of gold, he brought it to the boss at a *pay-yard* -- *T*his was where all the workers of the estate would meet for their daily assignments, and fortnightly, for their pay. The *pay-yard* was a former barrack when the boss's family owned slaves. There used to be several smaller houses surrounding a larger one at the *pay-yard*; but, when they had demolished the smaller dwellings, only the larger building remained. The slaves used to live in the smaller buildings and when the slaves were emancipated their dwellings were no longer needed. After the boss's parents had died the estate was inherited by him and his two siblings, who had since returned to Europe. The boss was left to manage the estate alone. The watchman had a sleeping-room at the rear of the larger building, but he was given a spot at the edge of the estate, and near one of the neighboring villages, to build a small house for his family.

Mr. Stanley Willis secured the treasures in his sleeping-room and went to tell the boss what he had found. The boss made him bring the treasures to boss's residence at a *great house* where the boss had said they would be better secured. For a very long time the boss had wanted to relocate the *pay-yard* to an area that was more accessible to a current main road. The *pay-yard* was at that time located in a remote area along an old route which had connected all the estates on the island to a main port of shipping. On the arrival of motor vehicles to the island, a more direct route to the port was constructed, and Mr. Scott wanted to move the *Pay-yard* to an area that was nearer to this new route; he was thinking about using the building's insurance to do so. The rest of his immediate family was then living in Europe. When his children were small, a nurse along with Mr. Scott's wife taught of them at home; but, as the children grew older, their parents wanted them to have a formal education, and didn't want to send them to any of the local schools. His wife had taken them to Europe and planned to return, but she found work in Mr. Scott's relatives' owned jewelry business in London and never did return home to the Caribbean. Mr. Scott began to make plans immediately to visit his family in Europe, and had instructed Mr. Stanley Willis to burn down the remaining large structure at the *pay-yard* while he was away in London. He had promised Mr. Willis that the transaction would be only between the two of them, and he wanted him to commit the arson in six months time -- right before Mr. Scott had planned to return to the Caribbean.

When Mr. Scott was leaving for London, he smuggled out the gold with him. He went by boat, and a former employee of his was then a custom officer, who was so proud of himself to meet his former boss that he didn't even check his luggage; in fact, he helped Mr. Scott to bring them on board. On his arrival in London, one of Mr. Scott's brother's friends was also a custom officer at the port of entry, and the friend was there along with several of Mr. Scott's relatives to welcome Mr. Scott to London. Mr. Scott had said that there was nothing to declare; and again, there was no search of his belongings. The London relatives had no problem handling the gold through their jewelry business, and they soon began to sell some expensive jewelry. Mr. Scott's wife wanted to become a partner in the family's jewelry store; but about four months after Mr. Scott had arrived in London, and before the new arrangement in the jewelry store had been completed, Mr. Scott received a telegram from Mr. John Young, another White man, whom he had left to oversee his estate in Tobago while he was gone. The telegram stated that the building at the pay-yard was totally destroyed by fire, and that Mr. Scott must return home at once. Another Black man, Mr. Kenneth Brown, was accustomed to manage the operation of the estate, even when Mr. Scott was around, so Mr. Young was serving only as a figure-head. Mr. Brown had closed up the building and gone for the day on the evening of the fire, when around 10:00 p.m. he was notified that the building was on fire.

"Where was the watchman?" he asked.

Mr. Stanley Willis's alibi was that he had gone to visit his family, and that some people had notified him about the fire before he could return to the *pay-yard*. However, he was held responsible, as he had neglected his duty. Messrs. Young and Brown were very hard on him, and immediately fired him from being the watchman.

Upon Mr. Scott's return to Tobago, Mr. Stanley Willis went to see him, and as soon as Mr. Scott saw him, he blurted out, "You fool; you can't count? -- I'd told you to wait six months, not four."

Mr. Stanley Willis told him that he thought he had counted six months. In the meantime the police were investigating the cause of the fire and Mr. Willis must stick to his story and say nothing about their conspiracy. It was concluded that a cat must have tripped over a kerosene lamp and set the building ablaze. Even though there was a nearby stream, in those days there was no organized fire department in the area, and once a fire had gotten out of control, all one could do was to watch the fire burn itself out. Mr. Stanley Willis wanted some money from his account with the boss; and also, he wanted some purchases from town for his family. However, the boss told him that all his money was locked away in a safe which was destroyed in the fire. That didn't sit too well with Mr. Willis who, perhaps for the very first time, spoke back to his boss in an unruly manner.

"Ah ha nuh job, nuh money; Mr. Peter Scott, whil yuh waiting fuh yuh insurance money, ina deh meantime, wha' yuh want meh and meh family fuh duh?" A few more heated exchanges between the two men took place before they saw Miss Ellen, a maid, looking through a balcony window of the *great-house*. Mr. Scott promised Mr. Stanley Willis to make arrangements for him to get his job back. However, Mr. Young the temporary caretaker and Mr. Brown the manager had already hired a watchman from Trinidad of East Indian descent to do Mr. Stanley Willis's job. Mr. Scott gave Mr. Stanley Willis a ten-dollar bill, and promised to find something else for him to do on the estate before sending him away.

CHAPTER TWO

On-Going Search for the Missing Treasures

MICKEY'S FATHER AND UNCLE continued to search the area of Engine Town for the missing treasures, and they would get together after work on week-days, and all day on week-ends to search for them. After a while everyone in the surrounding villages wanted to know what the men were up to. Mr. Stanley Willis had confided in his wife what he had found, and about the treasures which his boss had taken from him. Up to that point Mr. Stanley Willis still believed that the gold he had taken to the boss's home were hidden somewhere in the *great-house*. Now, Mr. Stanley Willis's wife and Miss Ellen, the boss's housemaid, were very close friends, and she told the housemaid what her husband had told her. When the boss had said that the treasures were destroyed in the fire; however, Miss Ellen had overheard the boss' conversation with the watchman, and felt that she had to do something to help out her friend and her husband: She had seen when a handyman, Amman, had loaded a very heavy chest into the boss's vehicle before the boss had left for London. After a conversation with Mr. Willis's wife, the maid Miss Ellen, and the handy man had a discussion about the treasures. Amman confirmed the maid's story and before long, people from the villages were searching along the river for more treasures.

Mr. Ramdeen, the new watchman, heard about the lost treasures, and one day as he was picking some pumpkin leaves from a vine along one of the river-banks he discovered another of the chest of gold. (He was a very strict vegetarian and would eat mostly the young pumpkin leaves and other vegetables. He also, ate the shoots of some young bamboos, and his wife would make different dishes with the fruits from two mango trees in the area.) As soon as he saw the chest, he thought that he knew exactly what it was. He broke open the chest, just to make sure that it was another chest of treasures. He brought it to his house where he began to make plan to return to Trinidad. He set up a shop in Arima and begun to make fine jewelry, a venture which went on to become one of the best jewelry manufacturing business in Trinidad.

Mr. Stanley Willis was rehired as the estate's watchman, and he continued to set fish traps along the river; all the time hoping that he would find more treasures. He had a set of traps close to the mouth of the river where the latter emptied into a bay. One Friday evening as the crew of a fishing boat was returning to shore, and had come near to the set of traps, the water suddenly became very turbulent. The boat capsized, and one of the fishermen, who couldn't swim, drowned. A distress call was sounded and people f locked to the bay, thinking the fishermen had made a large catch. (The fishermen were accustomed to sound conch shells whenever they wanted the villagers to come to the bay to buy fish.) The sea water at the shore continued to be very ruff all that evening and the villagers didn't recover the body. As they were looking along the bay well into the night, Mickey's uncle suspected that the boat which had capsized might have come to an area where another of the missing chests of treasures was, and whatever spirit was guarding the area, didn't want the treasures to be found.

Mickey's father and uncle were beginning to talk about abandoning their search, when Mickey decided that he would continue a search of his own without the adults knowing anything about it. He got Johnny, one of his friends from school, and they prepared some flash-lights, cutlasses and shoulder-bags before they set out to the area of *Devil Bambam Hole* in Engine Town. Mickey felt almost certain that the missing chests of treasures could be somewhere at that location. Up until that time, Mickey, his father and uncle still thought that there were the three of the chests still missing; they didn't know that Mr. Ramdeen had already found one of them. When Mickey and Johnny had come to where the mandarin tree had been uprooted and blocking the exit of the underground tunnel from *Devil Bambam Hole*, they made a clearance and entered the tunnel. It was really spooky inside and bats were flying everywhere. Some distance inside they came upon some drawings and writings along the tunnel's walls. They were trying to decipher the writings and hadn't noticed that their flashlight batteries were running low. The batteries soon went out, but much further along they could see a light beaming from the entrance of *Devil Bambam Hole*. As they were fumbling their way towards the light they could feel the breeze from the wings of bats which were whizzing pass their ears.

They finally came to a place where the entrance to *Devil Bambam Hole* was very high and directly overhead. The boys were hungry and tired, and the sides of the hole were too steep to climb. They cupped their mouths with their hands and began to shout, hoping that someone above ground would hear them and get help to come to their aid. After several hours they began to look at one another; both of them were thinking about the same thing: *We have no other choice, but to get out the way that we came in.* The bed of the tunnel was covered with gravel all along the way. If they follow the tunnel's bed, it was harder for them to get lost. They got on all fours and kept very close together, as they began their retreat. They had felt some huge boulders in the middle of the tunnel's bed as they were coming in, and hoped they wouldn't get hurt on one of those on their way out.

Their progress was very slow and pains-taking. Every now and then they stumbled upon a boulder. Mickey was leading the way, and at one point he felt something like one of the chest of treasures. He held on to it and Johnny came smack into him. The bats were everywhere. When they stopped advancing the bats began to bit them, and they bravely tried to fight them off. They had lost track of their progress, and didn't know how far they had advanced. They decided to tote the chest along, but they were very tired and hungry and had no idea how far to the exit they had come. Mickey began to think of what his father would say and do to him. *They finding one of the lost chests of treasures would surely appease his dad,* he thought and wasn't about to leave it behind. Johnny took off his shirt and while Mickey was hauling the chest, Johnny was fanning wildly about them in the darkness with the shirt. He then had more of his body exposed to the bats and they took advantage of it. In addition to their heads, the bats were now biting his chest and back. The situation could be likened to someone disturbing a colony of bees in their nest. After a heroic effort, they decided to leave the chest, and keep track of how far they would then have to travel before arriving at the exit, so they could know how far they would have to travel back when they return for the chest.

It was more than a day since they were gone, and back home their folks had become very concerned for the boys' safety. The folks organized a posse, and men from the villages on both sides of the river joined in. The police were called in, and while most of the men were searching along the river, Mickey's father and uncle focused their search on Engine Town. It wasn't known that the two men had brought the treasures to this area, and the brothers were still keeping it a secret, hoping that the boys would be found before someone come upon the missing chests of treasures.

After three days since the boys were gone, back at school all their friends were talking about them. It was very difficult for the teachers to keep order in their usual classes, and most of the time the pupils were told to get books from the cupboards and read them privately. By noon on the third day the boys finally had made it back to the village, but they refused to tell where they had been, and some adults, who were assuming that some evil spirit had over-taken them, insisted that they be not questioned. The police took them to a hospital for an evaluation, and treatment for many bat-bites, cuts and bruises they had sustained. They were kept for observation at the hospital before they were allowed to go home. Mickey's father and uncle visited them in the hospital and Mickey confessed to them where they had been; he told them everything about their ordeal.

"Ahyuh find wone ah dem!" his uncle exclaimed, before turning to his brother and said, "Ahwee hav tuh guh and get eit, fore somewone else beat ahwee tuh eit." They scolded the boys and told them that they mustn't share that information with anyone. It was already late in the evening, so they planned to set out at dawn the next day. Among the gears that they took along was a kerosene f lambeau to light their way in the tunnel and make a flame that was sure to drive off the bats. Mickey's father thought of, and walked along with, a roll of twine, which he tied to the mandarin tree before they entered the tunnel. He would roll out the twine by the way as they went along, and planned they follow the twine on their way out of the tunnel in case something should happen to their light and they find themselves in the dark.

"Hare yuh eis," said Uncle Timothy as they came upon the chest. The two men carried the load; each of them holding one end of the chest; while Mickey's father fended off the bats with the f lambeau in his other hand. They brought the chest of treasures safely out of the tunnel, and while they were resting they were discussing how best to secure the treasures until they could sell them. Uncle Timothy's best pal, Ossie, had recently returned to live in Tobago, after living in Trinidad for about ten years. However, each year during the season leading up to the national Carnival he would return to Trinidad to buy some exotic bird feathers which he used to make costumes for a masquerade band that he would put out each year since he came back to Tobago.

"Ah would guh tuh Trinidad wit' Ossie and bring alang ah sample ah deh gol tuh show tuh sume ah dem East Indian jewelers, an cee how much dey guh pay meh fuh eit," he told his brother.

"Al yuh duh, nuh leh dem try tuh get am fram yuh fuh nothing. Yuh hav tuh haggle wit' dem fuh com eup wit' ah good bargain," said Mickey's dad.

When Ossie was ready to return to Trinidad, Timothy went along with him, and after they had shopped for his exotic bird feathers, Ossie took him to Arima to sell his gold to one of the East Indian jewelers. They approached a few jewelry makers on the street before going into one of the established dealers. As soon as the jeweler and Uncle Timothy saw each other, right away each one recognized the other. Timothy used to work on the same estate in Tobago where Mr. Ramdeen was a watchman.

"Misa Ramdeen!" shouted Uncle Timothy.

"Timothy! Wha ina deh world brin yuh to Arima?" replied Mr. Ramdeen.

At that point Ossie stepped forward. "Wi want yuh to put ahwee eon tuh ah honest jewelry-dealer. Ahwee hav som gol fuh sale," he told Mr. Ramdeen.

"Yuh came to de right place. Ah mak' mi own jewelry; ah have mi own assay department wher' mi nephew working, and wi doesn't rob anybody. Wi have a good reputation round here," said Mr. Ramdeen.

Uncle Timothy showed him the gold and he said, "Right away ah can tel dat dis eis good stuff. How much eof dis duh yuh hav?" asked Mr. Ramdeen.

Uncle Timothy was looking at a chest that looked very familiar to him, and sitting over Mr. Ramdeen's counter; he replied while pointing to the chest, "Wi hav ah ches lik dat wone full."

Mr. Ramdeen's eyes opened very wide as he said, "Ah guh pay $2,000.00 dollars fuh dem. Eif al ah dem eis just like deh wone yuh want tuh sel meh, ah don't even hav tuh assay dem befor ah buy dem; dis eis really good stuff."

Uncle Timothy turned to Ossie to get his approval; in those days that was a lot of money. Ossie was more businesslike. "Leh wi shop around tuh cee ef wi culd get ah bettar deal," he told Timothy.

"Dem ader dealers guh rab yuh; dey wuld charge yuh al sort ah fees. Ah hate tuh cee yuh fellars get rab. Ah guh giv yuh $2100.00 dallars -- tak' eit or leav eit; Dat's meh final affah," said Mr. Ramdeen.

Uncle Timothy never dreamed to own so much money, and didn't want to pass up the deal. Mr. Ramdeen said, "Everybody round here going tuh ask yuh haw mach ah did affar yuh, befoe givin yuh ah price; dey know dat ah set deh standards and dat I is the bes' dealar raund; ah bet dat yuh won't get ah bettar deal.

Uncle Timothy was gazing at Ossie to figure out what he thought. -- "Now, yuh fellars will hav tuh mak up yuh mind," said Mr. Ramdeen. "Bring deh rest euf deh stuff tuh meh an yuh doe hav tuh wait fuh ah single day tuh get yuh money."

Ossie spoke up, "Wha eif yuh set ahwee up and ha som euf yuh boys ambush wi? Deposit deh money ina ah bank unda his name, and yuh car meet ahwee en Scarborough at deh port wher ahwee guh deliver deh gol tuh yuh. Wi guh giv yuh ah receipt statin dat yuh buy deh stuff fram ahwee. Yuh car bring alang witnesses tuh say dat weh deliver deh items tuh yuh."

"Dat's not how wi duh business; eif yuh fellas nat serious, duh wast meh tim. Yuh war tuh mak ah deal or not?" asked Mr. Ramdeen.

"Mi bigger brother, Issac, ha deh final say ina di matta,"said Uncle Timothy, as he and Ossie pretended to be about to leave.

"Ok; ah guh meet yuh fellars in Scarborough." Mr. Ramdeen looked at a calendar that was hanging from a shelf. "Wha' y'all think bout next Tuesday?" he asked.

"Dat shouldn't be any problem," said Uncle Timothy, holding the gold close to his chest.

"Ah guh giv yuh $200.00 eas ah deposit an yuh culd leav deh wone yuh hav wit meh," said Mr. Ramdeem.

Ossie was a bit short on the money he needed to buy some more of his exotic feathers. He turned to Timothy and said, "Tak' eit."

The two men took the money, gave Mr. Ramdeen the single nugget that they had and caught a taxi back to Port of Spain, where Ossie asked Timothy to loan him $100.00. They bought the exotic feathers from a fellow in Belmont, and after doing some more shopping, they were ready to return to Tobago. However, a boat wasn't leaving until 7:00 p.m., so they pass the time hanging out on Independence Square.

Mickey's father was pleased with the arrangement, and they decided to let Ossie into the transaction. On Tuesday the men met Mr. Ramdeen at the port at Scarborough. Mr. Ramdeen had brought along two nephews and he withdrew the money from a bank. Mickey's father and uncle opened a joint account, and deposited $1500.00 in it. In addition to the $100:00 that Ossie had borrowed, they gave him another $100.00. Everybody seemed satisfied, and in parting Mr. Ramdeen said, "Eif yuh fellas ha anymor gold fuh get rid eof, remember meh."

With their newly acquired *wealth*, Mickey's dad and uncle decided to take a few days off from work. In consideration for Mickey and his friend Johnny, the men decided to award each of them $50.00. The two brothers were then motivated to continue their search for the other missing chests of gold. Uncle Timothy thought of smoking out the bats from the tunnel at the Devil's Bambam Hole and making a thorough search of the tunnel without having to be disturbed by them. They gathered some dry coconut branches and set them afire at one end of the tunnel. Hundreds of bats came storming out of the tunnel near Devil Bambam Hole. When the tunnel was finally free of bats, the men entered it, each of them carrying a f lambeau. They searched every nook and cranny, but found nothing.

One day a woman was washing clothes in Edmond River at a place where a main road came to a bridge across the river. She had some grandchildren with her, and the bigger children left to look for mangoes and mandarins from trees which were located near the tunnel in Engine Town. There was a very small child, whom they had told to stay with their grandmother, but when the grandmother wasn't paying attention, the little child went after the older ones and got lost. Memories of the Mickey and Johnny's story were resurrected. People then believed that there was some evil spirit in the area and that it had something to do with the children's disappearance. Another search party was organized, and someone came upon the recent fire at the entrance of the tunnel. The police searched the tunnel, but did not find the child. The ash from the recent burnings at the entrance of the tunnel had caused everyone to believe that someone was practicing some evil rituals in the area, and that, indeed, the children's disappearance was connected to those rituals. The police sifted the ashes to find any possible human remains; but, they found none. They wanted to question anyone who was seen recently in the area.

Queenie had seen Mickey's father and uncle pass by her house several times on their way to the tunnel, but she didn't want to get involved with any police matter; therefore, she told them nothing. However, she told someone that she suspected the two men were up to some evil deed, and very soon whenever some people met them, the people would begin to sing:

Don't jealous them
Don't envy them
You never can tell
If dey get dey money fram deh devil in hell

About noon on the third, someone met the little boy sleeping on a culvert by a road that led from the tunnel, and they called off the search. The little boy didn't hear people calling out his name all during the days and nights that they were looking for him, nor was he disturbed by any vehicular traffic that had passed by on a nearby road during the time he was missing. The child's demeanor was very unusual, and again people thought that an evil spirit had overtaken him and refused to let anyone question him concerning his whereabouts.

CHAPTER THREE

An Evil Mystery

PEOPLE SUSPECTED THAT THERE was some evil mystery surrounding the disappearance of the children, and parents began to keep their children close to themselves. But, just as everything was beginning to return to normal, there was news of yet another missing child: A little girl's mother had left her at home with her siblings and had gone to wash clothes at Edmond River. The mother had gone to a place where the main road crossed the river at a bridge, but the little girl believed that her mother had gone to another location of the river, where women also used to wash, and where a boat had previously capsized some time ago as some fishermen were returning from sea. The people of Belle Garden and Glamorgan wasted no time in organizing another search party. While they were looking in Engine Town and around the areas they had searched for the previously missing children, a man found the little girl sleeping on a track-road that led to the river-mouth where the fishing boat had capsized.

At the river-mouth was a deep hole in the ground that had been dug several years before by a film company to be used in a scene of a movie, but after shooting the scene the film company had paid the owner of the property to fill in the hole with dirt; he pocketed the money and filled in the hole with coconut shells. During a subsequent heavy rain-fall, the whole area was f looded and the coconut shells f loated out of the hole and sailed away leaving the hole dangerously exposed. The danger was reported to the Government, but no official seemed to insist that the White landowner comply with their orders to fill in the hole. Children were warned that there was a danger of falling into the hole, to keep away from it, and to be supervised by an adult when the children were in the area. Learning that the missing girl was heading towards the hole when she fell asleep in the track-road, people began to ask one another, "What if she had gone as far as, and fell into, the hole?" Finally, Mr. Kenneth Brown, the estate's Black manager got the White land-owner's attention, and the hole was properly filled in.

About a month after the hole was filled in two teenagers were at that section of the river with their aunt. As she was washing, they were swimming in the sea. They had been in the water for very long and the aunt insisted that they get out, put on their clothes and go home. The older child obeyed his aunt, but the younger boy continued to linger on the beach. After he had remained on the beach for sometime playing in the sand, his aunt made him rinse off the sand from his body in the adjacent river, put on his clothes, and head for home. When she last saw him he had put on his clothes and was heading toward home, but he never reached there, and no one was able to account for him. They searched the area, but he was not found. When someone came upon the hole that was recently filled in with dirt, they called in the police, who ordered that the hole to be excavated to see if his body was buried in it; the investigation was negative. The youth was diabetic and was accustomed to have bouts of seizures. When he was about to have a bout he would begin to run aimlessly. With that information in their minds, the people didn't restrict their search for him to only the areas near the road which he would have had to pass to go home, but extended their search to cover all the areas through a neighboring coconut wharf, and along the river-banks. Four days after his disappearance some men from the Health Department who were working to control a proliferation of mosquitoes with insecticides along the river, found his body f loating upon the water.

It wasn't quite six months before another drowning occurred in the area: some siblings were sailing on a wooden raft when the raft capsized, and, when one of the girls found her-self in difficulty, her older brother tried to rescue her; but, he drowned, instead, while someone else was able to rescue his sister. That incident was followed by a woman who had gone to pick whelks, pachro, and other shell creatures off the rocks close to the shore of Edmond Bay. It was as if she had a premonition of her demise, because before the incident, she had stated to her companions that she hoped that nothing would happen to her; but, as she was prying a big whelk off a rock, and beneath the surface of the sea-water, a huge wave came and knocked her off the rock and into the sea. The last the others had seen of her was, when a huge wave was hauling her out to sea, and to a place where there was a big cave under the sea, and which tunneled inland beneath the rocks.

The villagers on both sides of the river held a joint meeting to discuss what seemed to be an evil mystery concerning the on-going missing children and other lost of lives in that area of the river. Mickey tried to convince his dad and uncle that the big f lood that had carried away the missing chests of treasures from the cave near Devil Bambam Hole might have carried some of the missing chests of treasures to mouth of Edmond River, and it was the ghost of a pirate which the Buccaneers had left to guard the treasures at Grandie River that was causing all the misfortunes. At the joint meeting Miss Ellen the boss's housemaid disclosed that Mr. Stanley Willis's wife had told her that Mr. Stanley had found a chest of gold along the river bed not very far away, and that he had turned the treasures over to his boss. Mickey's father and uncle believed that some of the missing treasures could've been carried by the rain runoff into the river and what Mickey was saying about a ghost guarding the treasures could be true.

The joint meeting concluded with the villagers deciding that they must get someone to exorcise whatever ghost was lurking in the waters around the river mouth and the bay. They contacted Mr. Gibbons, a Shouter Baptist leader from one of the neighboring villages, and they planned to meet at the river mouth on the first Sunday of February. Mr. Gibbons would have some of the ladies from his church to fast and sleep on the bare ground ("moan") inside his church for three weeks before the event, and after the exorcism there would be a baptism of any new believers. Mr. Stanley Willis and his wife were both Shouter Baptists, and so were Mickey's dad Isaac and his uncle Timothy. As news of the up-coming baptism spread, the event attracted many people. They witnessed the exorcism where there were flowers thrown into the water and lighted candles stuck in the sand, and Baptist members would speak in tongues while ringing bells, and passing out on the sand or in the water; some of them foaming in their mouths. Young Mickey and his friend Johnny were among the newly baptized members. When all the ceremonies were over, there were ten new members. However, when the dry season came around, the Government began to deliver water to containers that the villagers would put at the entrance to their houses for a supply of river water from a water truck. One Sunday some youths had gone spear-fishing and when they were returning home, as they came to Mr. Gibbons' house-entrance, one youth took aim at his container of water and shot a hole through it. As the youth was recovering the spear of his gun, Mr. Gibbons came up behind him and struck him over the head with a piece of wood. He ran off without the spear and did not seek any medical attention. Later that year he began to have severe headaches, and when they took him to a hospital, it was discovered that the blow had caused an abscess to form in his head and that it was too late to save his life.

Several months had passed between the time the youth was struck and the time of his death; therefore, no charges were brought against Mr. Gibbons. His funeral was well attended by many youths, who refused to let a hearse bring his casket to a cemetery. His friends would take turns bearing the casket by hand, while traveling on foot, and as the empty hearse drove very slowly in front of them. They had traveled a distance of about two miles and had to pass by Mr. Gibbons' residence on their way to the cemetery. When they had come to the location where the youth was struck, they stopped the hearse, rested the casket in it, and everyone gathered together to listen to speeches from various individuals. From there they formed two lines and marched behind the youths who were carrying the casket for about another half-a-mile, or so, to the Anglican cemetery. People associated this latest death with the evil mystery at the river, since it was Mr. Gibbons who had performed the exorcism. The incident brought a disgrace upon the Shouter Baptists and some people began to shun them. In revenge for their friend's death two youths from one of the villages destroyed Mr. Gibbons' plantain field one night. The field had just started to bear plantains when the youths chopped off the heads of the trees. Mr. Gibbons put everyone on notice that whosoever committed the felony would meet a tragic end of their lives as he was going to work obeah on them. One youth became afraid and confessed to the crime. The youths' parents paid Mr. Gibbons five dollars for every one of the plantain trees that was destroyed, and began to look for someone to keep away any evil spell upon their sons.

As time passed by, a donkey broke the rope by which it was tied to a tree. The animal went missing for more than a week, during which time one could hear some dogs barking near the river, but no one bothered to investigate the incidence. One day as Mr. Stanley Willis went to repair one of his abandoned fences across the river, he saw that the donkey had been trapped in quick-sand at a place where he used to store debris whenever he would repair the fence in preparation to set his fish-traps in the river. The debris which he had placed near the river-bank had caused quick-sand to build up near the river-bank, and soon grass began to grow in the area. The donkey went to graze on the grass and found it-self sinking in the quick-sand. There were signs that ass had struggled for a while before dying -- a large area of the quick-sand was disturbed. All four legs of the donkey were completely submerged in the quick-sand, and the animal's body was partly buried, also.

Mr. Ramdeen, Mr. Stanley Willis, Mickey's father and uncle, all seemed to be unscathed by the evil mystery. The men had some things in common: Mr. Ramdeen was a Hindu who believed in reincarnation and ancestral worship. He never left home without some fetish on his body or in his garments to ward off any evil spirits that might try to harm him. Also, he would display various religious f lags around, and, on the outside of, his house. Mr. Stanley Willis, Mickey's father and uncle, although they were Shouter Baptists had some beliefs that were quite similar to Mr. Ramdeen's: they, too, would attribute any mysterious event to an evil spell, which they could ward off by some religious relics, or memorized catch-words, and they would not leave home without a religious relic or rehearsing some psalms for their protection; they, too, displayed various flags around their houses.

The villagers weren't satisfied that Mr. Gibbons had done a good job in removing the evil mystery from the river. The slaying of the young man and the two youths that were led to destroy his plantain field seemed to be proofs of their conviction. They thought that Mr. Gibbons didn't really know what he had done, and 'twas all the more they should ostracize him. They decided to call in a Shouter Baptist leader from San Fernando, Trinidad to do another exorcism at the river. Mickey's father and uncle would accommodate him; but, various villagers agreed to put up a large contingent of members of his church that he had brought along with him from Trinidad. The Shouter Baptists from Trinidad were going to have another baptism after the new exorcism, and Mickey and Johnny were re-baptized. Also, the parents of the two boys who had destroyed Mr. Gibbons plantain field were urged to let their boys get baptized, too, in order to ward off any evil danger that might yet befall them. Just to be sure that everything was then okay, the Shouter Baptists from Trinidad remained in Tobago for a whole month, during which time he and his followers would go to the beach at Edmond Bay almost every day to bathe. They really enjoyed themselves, and their mission to Tobago seemed more like a vacation than a missionary event. The Tobagonians fed them well and all of their accommodations were free; besides those, they would hold meetings by the roadsides at night and collected an offering several times a week during those meetings. When their stay had come to an end, they promised to return to Tobago any time they were needed.

The search for the missing treasures had been suspended for quite a while, and Mickey's dad and uncle were then unemployed. They agreed with Mr. Stanley Willis that they should join company and search around his fences in the river and along the river-banks to find the missing treasures. They didn't know that Mr. Ramdeen had found one of the chests and the brothers told Mr. Stanley Willis that they had hidden four chests, but that two of them were still unaccounted for. The men become good friends and after each search Mr. Stanley Willis would share any fishes that he had caught in his traps with the brothers. Every now and then they would sight an alligator, but it would f lee before the men came close. In the meantime, Mickey and Johnny conducted searches of their own on weekends, or when there was no school. They would restrict their searches mostly to Engine Town and especially the area abound Bambam Hole. One day Mr. Stanley Willis suggested that they return to Grandie River and search it more thoroughly to see they could come upon any more treasures. Mr. Stanley Willis was a very good diver, and could stay very long below the water before he resurfaced to breathe. He surveyed the swamp's bottom very meticulously and almost inch by inch. After several weeks, and not finding anything, they abandoned the search at Grandie River, and again refocused on the areas around Edmond River where they suspected the missing chests might be.

Uncle Timothy helped Mr. Ossie to make costumes for the various masquerade sections of Mr. Ossie's band during the upcoming Carnival when he was not searching for the treasures, and one day Mr. Ossie announced that he would be returning to Trinidad to buy some additional fabric material and exotic feathers. In addition to Uncle Timothy, Mr. Ossie offer to take Mickey and his friend Johnny along. The boys were out of school and on vacation. They had never been to Trinidad before and were very excited about the trip. They planned to visit the Shouter Baptist's leader who had baptized them. In addition, Mr. Ossie had promised to bring them to Arima where there was perhaps the only remaining Carib settlement in Trinidad. Uncle Timothy visited Mr. Ramdeen and they were very glad to see each other again. When Uncle Timothy told Mr. Ramdeen how he was passing his time in Tobago, Mr. Ramdeen encouraged him not to give up his search for the chests of gold, as he could strike it rich by finding a worthwhile amount. He told Uncle Timothy that when he lived in Tobago, he didn't go looking for any gold, but instead, gold come looking for him, and how he found a chest of gold one day near the river, and right in his own backyard; this was the beginning of his success in the jewelry business.

Mr. Ossie took the boys to see the Carib settlement and they got to see how Caribs lived. Someone explained to them how the Caribs lived: their cultures, their occupations, et cetera. They still plaited mats and made other handcrafts out of local products; they fished and grew a lot of maze and cassava, just like Caribs about which Mickey had read in his history books at school. The boys' next trip was to San Fernando to see the Shouter Baptist leader who had baptized them and who reciprocated the hospitality he had received from Mickey's dad during the month he had spent in Tobago. It was during the Christmas season, and when they came back to Port of Spain there were many exciting things to do and see: as Mr. Ossie and Uncle Timothy shopped, the boys wandered about the streets and market place; they listened to debates by some vagrants in the parks; and they got to do some shopping of their own. In evening they took a taxi back to St. James at Mr. Ossie's cousin; the cousin's son had gone along with them.

They made more trips into the shopping center of the City by themselves during the following days. After two weeks in Trinidad it was time for them to go home to Tobago.

When Uncle Timothy got home, he told his brother that Mr. Ramdeen had found one of the missing chests, and that only one other chest was then unaccounted for. The brothers were able to find a little work with the Government during the holiday season, so they couldn't lend Mr. Ossie much help in preparing his masquerade costumes during that time. Right after the carnival, however, work slowed down and they didn't have to help out with making any more costumes for that year; so, they were free to search for last remaining chest full time. Mickey and Johnny conducted searches of their own; and, just as the adults, they wouldn't forget to carry along their religious relics to ward off any evil spell that might try to harm them. Their search was an ongoing one, and during which time they kept open ears to learn if anyone had found the remaining chest. They planned to continue their search until the chest was found. Uncle Timothy didn't have any children of his own, and he and his brother were saving the money that they had in the bank for Mickey to spend on his education when he got older, and it was for him to go off to college.

CHAPTER FOUR

Disruption within the Scott's Family

B ACK IN LONDON THE Scott's family members were disputing a division of the jewelry business. Based on an appraisal of the treasures her husband had brought to the business, Mrs. Scott was demanding a half of the entire business. However, her siblings felt that since it was their brother who had contributed the treasures to their business, Mrs. Scott was not entitled to an equal partnership. Moreover, they were wondering when she would be returning to her husband in Tobago: their children were growing up and had reached an age where they could take care of themselves without an adult's supervision. However, Mrs. Scott was encouraging her husband to sell off the property in Tobago and move to London, which he refused to do. Mrs. Scott moved out a house that she and her children had been sharing with one of her husband's relatives in London. Her oldest and youngest children were doing well at school; but, the second boy was beginning to develop disciplinary problems and would resist any one of his relatives that attempted to correct him. Mrs. Scott had hired a lawyer to work out the details of dividing the jewelry business, but now she needed him to intervene in various matters her second boy would have with the law. Then relatives eventually began to accuse Mrs. Scott of having an affair with the attorney.

Mrs. Scott decided to send the rebellious youth back to Tobago to be with his father which the son himself had said he would rather do. Mr. Scott would rather him stay in London and promised to go there and have a fatherly discussion with the boy and his mother. When Mr. Scott arrived in London, his wife told him that she was, indeed, having an affaire with the lawyer and that she did not want to break it off. However, she did not want a divorce from Mr. Scott. She wanted to divide the family jewelry business with his London relatives, and open a separate store which she planned to conduct with their children. Mr. Scott could join them if he would dispose of the Tobago estate and come to be with them in London. He tried to entice his wife to come back to Tobago by reminding her of the many banquets they used to put on at nights for the other rich White folks from Tobago and tourists visiting the island. She informed him that she had made up her mind and that she would remain in London. The division of the jewelry business was finally settled and based on an appraisal of the treasures from Grandie River, Mr. Scott would receive a half of the business; he would open a new store on behalf of his wife and children. When Mr. Scott was returning to Tobago he took along his second son to live with him and to give the youth a chance to clear his head and settle down. They came to Tobago and the only servants that had remained in the *great-house* were Miss Ellen and Mr. Amman; the others were no longer working there. The young man went from room to room in the house and memories of his childhood came flooding back to him. Out in a back lawn was an old silk cotton tree on which he and his siblings had tied a swing and used to have much fun. He lay down beneath the tree to do some quiet thinking: *the next day he planned to visit the pay-yard to see Mr. Stanley Willis.*

In morning his father drove him down to the *pay-yard*, but when they got there all the laborers had already gone out to the fields. The manager Mr. Kenneth Brown told him where he was most likely to find Mr. Stanley Willis. He took his father's shotgun and went in search of Mr. Stanley Willis who was in the river tending his fish traps and the youth crept up to the river-bank close to where Mr. Stanley Willis was in the water. He wanted to scare the watchman and fired a shot which skimmed the top of the water across river. Mr. Stanley Willis came running out of the river for his own gun, but the youth had hidden behind a coconut tree. After a while he came out and called out to the watchman who didn't seem very surprised to see him.

Mr. Stanley Willis said, "Paul Scott, ah hear yuh was comin back tuh

Tobago; yuh most grow up toh beh ah big man, but yuh wuldn't giv up yuh boyhod pranks. Ah membar how yuh used tuh lov tuh hang out wit meh, but ah busy now; when ah ha tim, ahwee guh sit down and talk, an yuh guh tel meh all bout Landan." Mr. Scott had told the youth that the watchman had found some treasures along the river, and the youth couldn't wait to know where Mr. Stanley Willis had found them. The watchman told him where he had found the chest treasures, and added, "Now, Paul Scott, ah know how yuh venturous, ber don't yuh guh lookin fer noh treasures ina dese watars, karse plenty of alligators rond hare."

The young man walked along the river on his way back to the *pay-yard*. He thought that *perhaps he may be lucky to find some treasures, too.* As he neared a bridge, he heard the voices of two boys coming from the river. They were Mickey and Johnny's; some years had past since the dreadful storm, but they had never lost hope of finding the remaining chest of treasures that had been washed away from the cave near Devil Bambam Hole in Engine Town. Paul wanted to scare them and fired a shot across the water ahead of them. They came running out of the river, picked up their clothes and ran off naked, while looking back to see who it was. Mr. Stanley Willis had warned them not to go near his fish-traps, and they thought that it was he who had fired the gun. They stopped running when they realized that it was Paul. The place where they were was not his father's property; and as such, Paul had no jurisdiction over it. Paul told them that it was his first day looking for treasures and that Mr. Stanley Willis had found a chest of treasures not too far away. The boys told him that they had heard of Mr. Stanley Willis's story and that ever since they had been looking for treasures, too. They decided to team up in their search the following day. Beside Paul having his father's shot gun, they decided to bring along some good luck charms for Paul to ward off any evil spirit that might try to harm him.

When Mr. Stanley Willis came into the *pay-yard* later that day, Paul was waiting for him. When Paul was small he loved to hang around the watchman who had thought him and his siblings many things, and Paul reminded him of the fun they used to have. He loved the way in which the watchman spoke, and the endless stories he used to tell him and his siblings. London was not as pleasant to Paul as being with the watchman. He said that he and his mother couldn't get along because she seemed to prefer his bigger brother and younger sister more than him, and it seemed as though he had to live up to his older brother's standard; whereas, his younger sister was allowed to set her own standard. He said that his father had planned to groom him to manage the estate, and he promised Mr. Stanley Willis a secured job. He didn't see a need to keep both the manager Mr. Kenneth Brown and a young woman who was keeping the books on the estate's business. He had studied book-keeping in London, and could handle the book-keeper's position. However, he wanted Mr. Stanley Willis to keep that a secret.

Mr. Stanley Willis said, "Dat ah lat ah figurin yuh hav tuh duh, Paul; yuh knaw? bur, meh believ dat yuh culd handle eit."

The next day Paul met Mickey and Johnny by a bridge along the main road. He was dressed in blue jeans and a course shirt which he had bought from London to wear when he went out into the fields of the estate in Tobago. He longed for a smoke of *grass,* a supply of which he used to get from the immigrants that had come to London from Jamaica. He had had runs-ins with the London Police over this issue, and his mother's lawyer would constantly intervene to get him out of trouble.

"You fellows know where I can get a supply of *pot?*" he asked Mickey and Johnny.

They had never heard of that term before, and asked if he was speaking of Mr. Stanley Willis's fish-traps.

"No; no," he said. "I mean *grass.* You may know it by the name *ganja. You* smoke it when you want to get *high.*"

They still didn't understand what he meant; so he asked, "Have you ever heard of marijuana? That's strange; I think all young people know about it. It's better than cigarettes and beer."

"Wi car m-e-e-t at deh foud market ah Scarbro dis comin weekend; som fellars fram Trinidad wuld bring tings tuh Tobago tuh sell. Dey might know wha yuh lookin fah," the boys told him. They also informed him of some evil spirits that were in the area, and gave him some relics they had brought for him to ward off any spirit that would try to do him harm. They searched the bottom of the river from the bridge up to where a tributary from Engine Town had joined Edmond River, and left off searching for that day.

The following day Paul wanted Mr. Stanley Willis to bring him to see the area of the old *pay-yard*. The place was over-grown with weed, but he could still some concrete pillars that had remained from the fire; and, as if they were peeping through the thick over-growth looking at them. Further along the road was an old bridge where horse-drawn carriages and other traffic would cross the river, and under which Mr. Stanley Willis used to help Paul and his siblings catch craw-fish which were hiding beneath the stones in the water. The place was let out by Paul's father to someone who was cultivating the area with fruit trees, sugar-cane and ground-provisions. As a part of the contractual agreement, the current occupant had planted avocados, oranges and other long term crops on the land. The avocados and oranges had started to bear fruits, and they had some fruits to eat and to bring back to the new *pay-yard*.

On Saturday morning when Paul's father was going to play the horses at the horse-racing at Shaw Park, he dropped Paul off at the intersection Main and Burnett Streets in Scarborough. Paul had said that he wanted to wander around the town to see how many changes were made since he had last visited it. However, that was just a ruse to meet up with Mickey and Johnny to look for someone who was selling *weed*. They met a stranger who told them to check out a Trinidadian who had a stall in the Scarborough market. Unsuspecting by them the stranger that they had met was an under-cover police detective who had been trying to arrest the Trinidadian at the market for drug-trafficking. The Trinidadian directed them to a couple at the back of a store in the Town-bay area, and in front of Botanic Garden, where they could make arrangements to have a supply of marijuana from Trinidad.

The police detective was at the port when a steamer, which commuted between the islands on semi-weekly schedule, arrived in Tobago from Trinidad the next Tuesday morning, and he trailed the Trinidadian to the residence in front of Botanic Garden. Later that morning when Paul went looking to buy some marijuana, he stood out like a sore thumb. White

People were not accustomed to hang around that area. When Paul had left the back of the building, and he was waiting at some refreshment booths by the front of the building for his father to pick him up. The detective approached him and asked to see what was in his pockets, and Paul was arrested for dealing with a controlled substance. He was later released in the custody of his father. The detective who made the arrest and laid the charge named Constable Bascombe. In court at a trial, Paul's father had retained one of the most brilliant barristers from Trinidad. The detective in laying the charge had misspelled the name *marijuana*, and the barrister asked him, "Detective Bascombe, you laid the charge against my client, how long have you been a detective? And from whom did you receive your training?"

Detective Bascombe said that he had been a detective for ten years, and that he was trained by his supervisor.

Barrister: "Have you ever arrested anyone for possession of marijuana before? Tell the court what is marijuana, and how is it harmful."

After the detective had given a long explanation, the barrister asked him, "Detective Bascombe, have you ever done any research of your own on marijuana? The barrister handed him a *Miriam Webster English Dictionary,* and said, "Tell the court what is the dictionary's definition. After searching the dictionary for about five minutes, the detective said, "Sir, it is not listed in the dictionary."

The barrister remarked, "You said that you were trained by your supervisor; if your supervisor had told you to jump over a bridge, I can bet you wouldn't have done so. I'm putting it to you that marijuana is listed in that dictionary, and that the only reason you couldn't find the word is because you don't know how to spell it correctly. Your honor, I move that this case be thrown out of court because the officer has proven himself to be unreliable."

Paul won his first brush with the law in Tobago. However, he was addicted to marijuana, and relied on his father's high status in the community to get out of any trouble that he might find himself in. But, once one have had a brush with the law for any drug activity in those days, whether one win or lose, there would be a stain upon one's character, and the police would always be upon one's trail. Therefore, Mickey's father said to Mickey, "Ah doe war yuh guh hangin eout wit dat bway any moh. Eif was yuh deh police hold wit drug, al dis tim yuh bin rottin ina jail --wone law fuh deh rich an wone fuh deh por. Forget bout deh gol wha missin, wone day som lucky person guh fine eit. Ina deh meantim, jus tink bout yuh futha."

Mr. Stanley Willis said, "Paul Scott, ah knows dat yuh eis yung, ber yuh ha yuh whol futha head eof yuh. Settle down and mak' somethin eof yuhself. Yuh tell mi dat yuh culd keep book and yuh plan tuh tek ober deh offic fram deh gal ah deh *pay-yard*, and dat yuh and meh guh run deh estate. Eif dis eis deh way yuh plan tuh carry eon, betah yuh fadar sen yuh back ah England fuh beh wit yuh modar."

Miss Ellen and Amman also counseled Paul: "Doe embarrass yuh fadar," said Miss Ellen, "yuh fadar culd mak arrangement fuh deh vehicle licen inspectar fuh com and giv yuh ah drivin tes rite arn dis estat, and wen yuh ha deh licene, yuh and meh culd duh deh shoppin pan weekend, and leh yuh por fadar rest up."

Amman, who was shaking his head in agreement, added, "Sometimes meh, tuh, culd com long fuh deh ride and tuh lif anyting dat's tuh heavy fuh aryuh tuh cary. Paul, yuh culd hah ah brite furtah. Eit ha odar White bways yuh age down ah low side dat yuh culd associat wit' and leave dis drug business lone."

Paul did not see Mickey and Johnny since his trial. Mickey and Johnny, being mindful of Mickey's father's advice, were avoiding Paul. Paul had already had some driving skills from London, so his father made arrangements for the motor vehicle inspector to come to the *pay- yard* to examine Paul and to give him a Trinidad and Tobago license. In the meantime, Paul would hang out with the girl in the office, and help her with the book-keeping. Each day Mr. Stanley Willis would make time to chat with him. One day he said to Paul, "Paul Scott, wen yuh tel meh dat yuh culd kep bok, at fus, meh nuh beh believ yuh; bur, tuh cee eis tuh behliev: Meh nuh neber hare yuh fadar, nur Misa Kenneth Brown, nur deh bok-kepa, sah yuh mak ah mistak yet: Yuh doin fine pan am, Paul Scott".

Paul's father would not let him take the car out by himself, except he was driving about on the estate. And, on the estate Paul was not allowed to drive the family's car very much, but would rather use a tractor trailer with which the laborers used to bring coconut and cocoa from the fields. The main reasons Paul's father wanted Miss Ellen or Mr. Stanley Willis to be with the youth whenever he was driving in the public domain was to ensure that the police did not harass him; but also, to see that Paul kept away from marijuana. Mickey's father, in the meantime, would remind Mickey of plans that they had for Mickey to study abroad, and any infraction upon his police record would make it difficult for him to get a visa to travel. Before Mickey had graduated from elementary school, he went on to high school, while Johnny waited until he had almost graduated from elementary school before becoming a carpenter's apprentice; and, as time passed, their friendship weaned and they gave up searching for the missing treasures.

CHAPTER FIVE

We Are Living in a Small World

U PON FINISHING HIGH SCHOOL, Mickey applied for admission to a university in the United States of America and was accepted. However, he must obtain a visa in order to go to America. He was given an appointment at the United States Consulate (U.S.) in Port of Spain, and he went into Scarborough to buy a ticket to take a night ferry to travel to Trinidad. After buying the ticket, Mickey was waiting to catch a bus to get back home, and as he looked down a street, he saw Paul driving his father's land-rover, and coming towards him. Mickey evaded him and ran behind a store. Paul had escaped the observation of Miss Ellen and Mr. Stanley Willis and was desperately looking for someone who could help him to get some marijuana. Mickey had heard that Paul still had a drug habit, and wanted to evade him. After a long while Mickey came out from behind the store and waited at another bus-stop for his bus.

As he was waiting he observed a man installing a large pane of glass on the display window of a jewelry store. The next day, after Mickey had had his interview, and got a visa to go to school in America, as he was passing by the Queen's Park Savannah, he met Wendell Blake whom he had known from Tobago. Wendell and his siblings used to attend the high school that Mickey attended, but that whole family went to live in Trinidad before some of the children had finished high school. In fact, Mickey had a crush on Wendell's younger sister. Mickey inquired about the other siblings and was told that Wendell's bigger brother had become a bank executive after the bigger brother had obtained his bachelor's degree from a local university; his two sisters were still attending a university in

Canada; however, Wendell, was on drugs, and had no ambition to move on to make something of himself: he was out of work and would loiter around the Queen's Park Savannah panhandling from people going to, and coming from, the U. S. Embassy. Wendell told Mickey that his dad had lost his job as a government's communication officer who used to present educational f lims to various community groups in the evenings. As Mickey was leaving, he said, "Can yuh spar meh ah qartar?" and an old lady who was selling mangoes at a stall beneath a tree shouted, "Doe giv eim. Des bways duh nothin, ber use drugs an harass people a-l-l day lang." Mickey arrived at Mr. Ossie's cousin home in St. James, and as he was leaning over the railing of a porch, he saw a gentleman walking up a hill towards him. "Didn't ah cee yuh installing ah pane ah glass buh wa jewelry store ein Tobago yesterday?" Mickey asked him.

"Yuh sure did; eis ah lucky ting ah didn't commit ah crime, and yuh wasn't deh police lookin fuh meh," the man replied. "Ah was in Tobago fixin up ah new sto-r-e fuh Ramdeen. Ah jus gat aff deh plen right dis minute, an tek ah taxi ina town; ah livin jus at deh tap eof dis hill," the man added.

After Mickey arrived in New York and had taken a few classes at his new school, one day during lunch-time he had gone to a post office to buy some stamps and to mail some letters back home to let his folks know how he was fairing. He was amazed at the way the other customers had queued-up very orderly as each patron waited his turn at the counter; he had noticed the same thing at the bus stops. The person right in front of him was a body-builder, and right away Mickey recognized him.

"Samuel Lewis?" Mickey asked.

And the body builder turned around and replied in return, "Wher yuh know meh fram? Are yuh fram Trinidad?"

"No," Mickey said; "Ah fram Tobago; bur, ah used tuh cee yuh and meh fus cousin husband ein deh newspapers al deh tim eas yuh enter various bady buildin exhibition."

"And, yuh mak' meh out fram only deh pictures? Eit es ah smal world dat weh livin ein," said the body builder.

Samuel Lewis had a gold ring on each of his fingers, and Mickey said, "Ah cee yuh eis ah man eof gold."

"People always admiah meh rings; yuh knoh? Ramdeen fram Arima made dese. Meh sistar liv nat tuh far way fram heh stor ein Arima, and ebery tim ah guh tuh cee sheh, man, ah must pas ina Ramdeen. Deh man eis competin gainst dem big stor-e-s lik Y deh Menis and heh holdin heh own. Al heh children dem was ein deh business; bur, now som ah dem ein school ein Englan, adars ein America, or ein Caneda. Wha' was yuh fus cusin husban nam?"

"Albert Moses," said Mickey.

"Bway, Albert eis meh g-o-o-d padner; heh an meh used tuh wok out ina ah gym ein Belmont, Port eof Spain ein deh evenin," said the body-builder.

"Wone euf meh uncle friend beh tak meh an meh frend Johnny tuh Ramdeen befo. Ein fac, meh fadar an meh uncle sel em som gold. Dem Caribs stil livin ein dey villige ein Arima?" Mickey asked; "deh same uncle friend beh tak wee tuh cee how dey livin; eis jus eas weh beh read ein weh readin bok ah school."

They had come to the cashier, and the body-builder transacted his business, and left after bidding Mickey good-bye. Mickey was relieved because he didn't want to be asked about his cousin's whereabouts: She had come to America, and planned to sponsor her husband when she had settled down, but she didn't sponsor him, and Mickey knew that the husband had lost contact with her.

Mickey took chemistry classes and hoped to get a job in a laboratory upon his graduation from school. While he was still in school he met an American boy whose mother and father were the administrators of two different hospitals. And, the American was able to get his mother to find Mickey a part-time job in one of the hospitals. One evening when he had gone to prepare a patient for surgery the next day, as soon as Mickey opened his mouth the gentleman asked, "Where are you from?"

When Mickey had said "Tobago." The patient replied, "My family was originally from Tobago, but we moved to Trinidad when we children were still small; we finished elementary school at the Richmond Street School right by the river in Port of Spain."

Mickey replied, "Dere's nuh riber aon Richmond Street."

"Yes; dere's deh big riber runnin right behind deh school," said the old man.

Mickey didn't press the point as he wasn't quite familiar with Port of Spain; however, when he had gone home that night, he was thinking about the discussion he had had earlier that evening with the old man, and he remembered that he had read in his history books at school, where the Government had used mule carts to transport dirt from Laventille Hill to fill in a river running through the city and had diverted the river to Morvant; and also, the city was enlarged in the Wrightson Road area around the same time. Mickey went to visit the patient the next evening and told him about his recollection. The gentleman told him that he had left Trinidad many years ago to work on the construction of the Panama Canal and when there was an outbreak of malaria in the Canal Zone, he came to the United States to get treatment. He married an American woman and they lived on Bergen Street in Newark, New Jersey until his children were grown. He and his wife were divorced in 1945, and after he had become blind he went to live with one of his married children.

The hospital staff seemed to be referring all incoming male patients from the Caribbean to Mickey. The patients spoke with a thick West Indian accent, and often they were misunderstood. About a week after Mickey had met the first patient, he had to tend to another patient from Trinidad, who was originally from Kendal, Tobago and not very far from where Mickey grew up; and, he and Mickey bonded well. When he was being discharged from the hospital he gave Mickey his address and telephone number, and an invitation to visit him at home. Mickey was excited and told a woman at whose home he was living about the invitation. That latter patient was a semi-retired physician, whose brother turned out to be a former head-master of an elementary school that the woman had attended in Trinidad. The woman was very exited and urged Mickey to visit the physician. When Mickey arrived at the physician's, after introducing Mickey to his wife, the physician and Mickey retired to the basement of the house, where the physician had a room modeled as a Caribbean resort: There was a huge pond which was recycled by a water-pump via a fall. The pond was reminiscent of the swamp called Grandie River, and the water-fall reminded Mickey of Kendal Water-fall; the walls of the room had huge paintings of beaches with coconut trees and men tending to their fishing boats. The physician told Mickey that he had an artist painted the scenes from pictures he had taken when he had gone back to Tobago to visit many years ago. He also said that, that was the room where he went to relax when he was feeling tense, and that he would spend many hours there while making plans for the future: he was planning to go back to Tobago, buy a piece of land near the sea and build a casino.

While he was telling Mickey about his future plans the front door-bell rang, and he went to let someone in. His wife was diabetic and was a leg-amputee. He returned with a beautiful young woman, whom he introduced to Mickey as his secretary. He said that they had some private business to discuss, and told Mickey to go up-stairs because his wife might have something for Mickey to eat. His wife gave Mickey some ice-cream and cake, and after he had eaten the refreshment, Mickey called out to him to say that he was leaving because he had to go to work. That Sunday evening when Mickey went to work there wasn't very much to do, and he had gone to relax in a solarium where he met yet another patient from the Caribbean; this one from the Island of Dominica. As they were talking, the man told Mickey that he knew the physician, and that he had done much handyman work for the doctor: it was he who had put together the model resort in the basement for him. Then he began to tell Mickey some gossips about the doctor and his wife: he said that the doctor used to go off vacations with the secretary, the wife had frozen his bank-account, and that much of the doctor's money was tied up in court.

As their conversation continued, the Dominican told Mickey that when he had first come to America, he married a blonde White woman whom he had met one night in a bar in New York City. Their marriage was going quite well, until one evening he went home and couldn't find his wife. That was quite unusual as his wife wasn't accustomed to go out, without first telling him where she was going. As he lay in bed worrying that something might have happened to her, about 11 p.m. she came home with her hair dyed jet black. He said that he was so enraged, he asked her, "Ded yuh kno dat eis cause yuh blond wha mak meh maried yuh?" Their argument became very heated and he struck her, whereupon she called the police and he was arrested. He called the physician who was his doctor to bail him out jail, and he and the doctor had become very good friends ever since. He was divorced and didn't plan to ever get married again. He was then living alone and whenever Mickey would cook a Caribbean dish, he would bring him some food while he was in the hospital. They lost touch with each other after he was discharged from the hospital.

At the beginning of each semester during registration, all students were required to pay a mandatory fee for the students' extra curricular activities which were carried out by the various approved student associations. Mickey would skip much of those functions, as he had to work to support himself. However, one year at Christmas time all the students from the various islands were recoding greetings to be sent to radio stations back in their home-lands to broadcast over the air, and one of Mickey's friends from Trinidad and Tobago had told Mickey that he must go and record some greetings to his relatives and friends. Moreover, Uncle Timothy had told him that he must sent and tell him how he was enjoying the white Christmas. Mickey remembered with nostalgia how when he was still at home in Tobago, they used to gather around the radios when these greetings were being broadcast, to hear if any of the greetings was coming from someone that they knew. He was sure to mention Mama Celina his grand-mother, Uncle Timothy, his younger brother and sister Selwyn and Donna, and *to give a shout out* to some of his boyhood friends by names.

The weather back then seemed to be much more severe than now-a-days; and whereas, many students from the Caribbean seemed to boast about enjoying their white Christmases, Mickey hated them. After school, whenever he had to work in the evenings, he would get off work at a time when the buses ran every hour. When he had to work until midnight, he would miss the midnight bus, if it were running on schedule. Therefore, he used to get off work five minutes early, until he was reported by a clerk one night. He was reprimanded; and after, whenever he missed the mid-night bus, he would walk home, and often got there before the one o'clock bus would pass. When it was very cold outside, as his body began to warm up by the temperature within his home, it would tingle; and it felt as if his head were a block of ice; it would hardly have any feelings at all. Besides the cold elements Mickey faced many other dangers. There were times when he almost got shot: One night the police were responding to a domestic quarrel, and Mickey was waiting for the bus under an awning at the front of a store, adjacent to the doorway to the apartment where the dispute was, when two White police officers come towards him with their guns drawn. Another time as he was hurrying from one street to another to catch a bus, a police car came towards him loaded with White officers. After stopping and questioning him, he recognized one of the officers in the rear seat who would moonlight at the hospital on some evenings. That officer said something softly to the others and they let him go, claiming that they were responding to a call that someone fitting Mickey's description was trying to break into a U.S. postal mail-box. Another night a woman had just gotten off a bus, and as Mickey was hurrying to get home, the woman pulled a gun on him. He shouted, "Mis, doe shoot. Ah aint troublin yuh; ah jus gat aff wok an mar hury fuh gat hom; ah hah tuh gat eup early ein deh marnin."

The woman said, "Mister, don't you ever come sneaking up on me like that again."

On yet another night as Mickey was walking home he saw three youths walking in the street and they were going in a direction opposite to the one he was traveling. When they almost met him they split up: one of them entered the center of the road, another went on the opposite side of the street, while the third continued to come towards Mickey; he was almost surrounded! He put his back against a fence, and while holding his brief case with one hand, he reached under the breast pocket of his coat with his other hand, pretending to have a weapon, and halted. The youth that was coming towards him joined the one in the center of the street, and when all three of them had passed him, Mickey ran; he ran all the way home.

While working in the hospital he had seen several victims of a mugging come through the Emergency Room. Before those crimes were brought under control, the conditions were almost unbelievable. Almost every evening there used to be two or three cases of a mugging. Most of the visitors who came to see the patients were from out of town. The hospital was a specialized one and consolidated about ten years before, and though the doctors had practicing privilege at that hospital, their offices were located in the suburban areas and most of their patients were suburbanites. The State had funded the consolidation of the hospital, equipping it with the most modern state-of-art equipment.

People used to joke about three dollars being *'muggers' money'* and sometimes when one person would ask a coworker for a loan to buy something from the cafeteria to eat, his coworker might say, "I'm broke, also; the only money that I have is *'muggers' money.*" If a mugger held a person up and the person had less then three dollars, the mugger would beat the person up for not having enough money and for wasting the mugger's time. It would seem as if the muggers dare anyone to walk the streets at night, no matter how big the person was. One night an orthopedist called Mickey and another fellow from Porto Rico to assist him to reset someone's arm; the person had been mugged. The fellow who was from Tobago was very huge and about six and a half feet tall. He said he had been walking on a street, when two men and woman 'jumped' him. After they had passed him, the woman who had an umbrella closed with something heavy in it, struck him with the umbrella at the back of his head. The two men, each taking one of his arms, pulled one of his shoulders out of its socket. The orthopedist placed a folded sheet under the patient's injured shoulder, with that arm extended sideways; and with Mickey holding one end of the sheet, while the Porto Rican holding the other end, the doctor told them to act as if they were raising the sitting patient off a chair; and he slipped the shoulder back into its socket.

CHAPTER SIX

They Had Come a Full Cycle

B EFORE MICKEY HAD FINISHED college he had hired a lawyer, who helped him to change his United States immigration status, and upon his graduation he was able to be interviewed by various companies that had gone to his school to interview prospective new employees. He was hired as a laboratory technician by a chemical company who manufactured catalysts for the petrochemical industry and made air pollution control devices for motor vehicles and various industrial machineries. In the meantime, the German owner of the company had gone to South Africa where he had met an English man who was managing a diamond and other precious metals company. The German owner invited the English man to come to America and take charge of one of the divisions of his company. After about six months in America, the English man in turn sent to South Africa for someone whom he used to teach London, and whom he had previously sent for to work for him in the South Africa precious metal industry. That former student was none other than Henry Scott, who had left Tobago with his mother and siblings to attend school in England. He then had a Ph.D. and was sent for to come to America to manage the precious metal laboratory where Mickey had been working. Mickey had remembered the name Henry Scott; but, he and his new boss didn't recognize each other. They had much to discuss.

Henry had acquired an interest in precious metals from their jewelry business back in London, and decided to study Chemistry at college to be able to analyze various products in the precious metals in their business. However, Mrs. Scott was inflicted by breast cancer, and her lawyer friend had gone out of her life while Henry was still in college. When Mrs. Scott succumbed to her illness, Mr. Scott and Paul went to London to attend the funeral. Paul seemed to have missed her the most of all her children, and he went into a deep depression that caused him to increase his craving for drugs; her daughter was unable to manage their jewelry store properly, so one of Mr. Scott's siblings bought the business, and incorporate in into Scott's original jewelry store.

Back in Tobago, a severe tropical storm had destroyed most of the large estates, and some of them went bankrupted. Mr. Scott and Paul bought a set of heavy equipment and began to do landscaping for the other large landowners. They moved out of the *great house* and rented a house in the Scarborough. Miss Ellen, Amman and Mr. Stanley Willis would upkeep the property at the *great house* which they were then renting out for various conventions, parties, weddings, and those sorts of things. Paul still loved to get *high* on marijuana. In fact, he had moved on to more addictive drugs and would attend gatherings at the *great house* and some other places where he would look for someone to sell him drugs. Most of the youths in Tobago knew that he was a drug-user and would crave his company. Mr. Stanley Willis kept an eye on him and tried to get him to give up using drugs; but, it seemed like a waste of time. Beside drugs, Paul craved the attention he was getting from some young people. Whereas, other White youths discriminated against the other races in Tobago, it was as though Paul were color blind.

Henry Scott was very concerned about his brother and asked Mickey to write his father, uncle, Mr. Ossie and anyone else they knew who could get his brother some help. An acquaintanceship with Mickey's relatives already existed from the days Paul used to hunt for the lost treasures with Mickey and Johnny, so when Mickey wrote to ask for his relatives' assistance with Paul, his uncle Timothy immediately sent to call for Johnny. Mr. Ossie was beginning to prepare for his band of masqueraders, and besides he had set aside a piece of land on which he planned to start a *steel-band tent*. Uncle Timothy wanted Johnny and Paul to go to Trinidad with Mr. Ossie to buy some steel drums from an oil company, and to find a steel-pan tuner who would teach future band members how to play pans, as the pans were being tuned. Paul was glad to participate; this was an opportunity for him to buy some drugs for himself from someone in Port of Spain. Uncle Timothy had told Mr. Ossie to guard Paul carefully, and he did. Mr. Ossie ended his mission to Trinidad without Paul getting himself into any trouble. When they returned to Tobago Paul was with the *pan-tuner* and future band members as the pans were being tuned, and he learned to play all the tunes the pan-tuner thought. What he looked forward to most was the cooking they used to do on an outside fire by the pan tent. He loved the stewed crabs and roasted breadfruits or some very broad wheat-flour dumplings the boys used to have almost every day. His father was very angry at Paul's latest behaviors and barred him from coming into his house. Miss Ellen and Amman were instructed not to let Paul come around the *great house*, and Mr. Stanley Willis was to leave him alone and let him reap the consequences of his actions. However, they would hide as they went against Mr. Scott's orders. Miss Ellen was especially pleased when Paul started to see a Black girl from one the neighboring villages. She would often give Mr. Stanley Willis food to bring to him and his girlfriend. When Paul was not assisting Mr. Ossie in making costumes for his masquerade band, he was learning to *beat* pan, and his girl-friend was right there beside him. Eventually, she began to learn *to play* pan, too.

During the carnival, his girlfriend *played mass* only on Carnival Monday and *beat pan* on Tuesday; while he *beat pan* both days. At that point marijuana usage had grown in Tobago, and on Carnival Days the police seemed to be always looking the other way as someone was *getting high off a joint*. Paul smoked to his heart's content. Once as he was having a good time, he turned around to hear Mr. Stanley Willis begging him *not to let down his father anymore*. Mr. Stanley Willis had gone into Scarborough, not so much to see the various bands, as much as to keep an eye on Paul, and to ensure that he did not get into trouble with anyone. On Carnival Tuesday night Paul stayed with his girlfriend at the servants' quarters at the *great house*, and she was found to be with child shortly afterwards. The first person he told was Miss Ellen, who told Amman. They didn't want Mr. Stanley Willis to know about it, least he would tell Mr. Scott. However, Mr. Scott learnt about it, and that the girlfriend gave birth to a son, and he was furious with Miss Ellen and Amman. About ten years later, Paul's girlfriend's sister who was in America assisted her in being sponsored as a domestic servant to an American woman, and later the girlfriend brought her little son to the United States. After the boy had completed high school, he joined the United States navy and traveled to various foreign countries like England and Germany.

Back at Mickey's job at the laboratory, he received several promotions for which he gave credit to his boss Henry Scott. Henry would send him to various seminars; he learned how to prepare various samples for analysis, and to determine different amounts of precious metal in a solution by plasma. And, when a newer machine was being used, he would learn to determine the amount of precious metals in a solid sample by X-ray Fraction (XRF). One year they were having a Christmas party at the general manager of the refinery home, and as it approached eleven p.m. and they had already given out various awards and Christmas gifts, it was announced that Henry Scott, whose wife was not at the party, would be resigning his position in the laboratory and returning to London with his family. He said that his wife was home-sick and wanted to go home. However, the truth was that Henry's behavior had changed dramatically. He had moved away from acting as a *perfect English gentleman* to someone who was trying to out do the Americans in cursing and drinking. The general manager used to cuss, and every other word in any of his conversations was an obscene word. Most of the people who worked under would try to imitate him and cussing had become a part of the company's culture. His co-workers used to laugh whenever they heard Henry Scott cuss; it just didn't sound right and as if he was forcing himself to do it: his demeanor remained very pleasant and his cuss-words seemed to be out of place in his sentences. Some people started to leave the party, but, Mickey had forgotten his hat, and returned to the party just in time to hear the general manager announced, "Now that all the women and other minorities have left, you fellers are free to say anything you want." There was a big laughter from the others. The next year, when it was time for promotions within the company, Mickey was promoted to be the Laboratory Supervisor and given a large increase in salary. Milton Simms the person who had taken Henry Scott's place as Laboratory Manager told Mickey that Henry Scott's last words to him before he left, were to make sure that Mickey got a promotion that year because he was an excellent worker.

When the family returned to London, Henry Scott went to teach at his Alma Mater; a day his wife was in a supermarket, when she ran into a person who was the Principal of an elementary school where she had taught before she went to South Africa. He was very glad to see her, and after a very long conversation, he invited her to reapply for a teaching job at the school. Their children had mixed feelings coming back home: First, they missed the new friends they had made in South Africa. And, then they felt they had to be missing new friends all over again; they really loved the Americans. They were glad they didn't sell their house in England, and went to live in their former neighborhood. Most of their English friends were still around, and they had much to tell them about the places to which they had been, and about their experiences overseas.

The Ramdeen's family, meanwhile, was climbing up the social ladder: His older son had gone to school in Florida and become an architect, his second son had completed medical school in Canada and his oldest daughters had gone to law school in London, while the younger one took up accounting. While the doctor was visiting his sisters in London, someone sent him on a blind date. That date was with Sandra Scott, Henry's youngest sibling! They *hit it off,* got engaged and were married. Henry gave *her away,* and Mr. Ramdeen and some of his relatives had gone to England for the occasion. Old man Scott, the bride's father, had suffered a massive stroke previously and was then confined to a nursing home in Tobago; so, his relatives were very careful to conceal the wedding from him, not knowing how he would take it.

Mr. Ramdeen provided a wedding ring for his son and was very proud of his design. Sandra Scott's aunt reciprocated with one from her store. The doctor did two more years of post- graduate studies in England before he and his wife returned to Trinidad where he accepted a position with the Government as a District Medical Officer (DMO). After five years on the job, he was transferred to Tobago to become the Senior Medical Officer of a hospital on that island. In addition, he was allowed to pursue a private practice to supplement his sub- standard salary from the Government. Sandra had gone to see her father a few times since she had returned to Trinidad; and there wasn't much he could do, but to respect her decision to marry out of her race. During his last days, she and her children would visit him in the nursing home. The doctor had helped Paul to get some help with his drug addiction, and when his father passed away, Paul was left in-charged of the *great-house* and landscape business. Henry and his wife had come home from England to attend his father's funeral, and the siblings were reunited after several years. Mickey would've liked to there to support the siblings, but was unable to do so; therefore, he sent a telegram to them expressing in deepest sympathy.

The doctor had political aspirations and planned to run for elective office as a candidate for the Opposition Party, and anyone, who was working for the Government and wanted time off from work with pay, would go to him for some sick-leave; he would ask the person, "How many days off do you need?" The sky was the limit: he wanted to show inefficiency in a government, which he would constantly be preaching against. He ran for election and lost to a seasoned office-holder. In retaliation for his opposition to the Government, he was transferred to a remote district on the island, which was, in a sense, a demotion. On weekends he would go scuba diving in the sea off the coast of Tobago, and one weekend he drowned at sea. His body was found two days later, having been washed up on a neighboring beach. He was cremated on one of the banks of a river in Trinidad.

When Henry telephoned Mickey to tell him about his brother-in-law's drowning, Mickey decided to attend the funeral. It was the first time he had been back to Trinidad and Tobago in several years. The Ramdeen's daughters also f lew in from London for the occasion; their brother, the architect, was already in Trinidad and was then working for a large Chinese construction company. Mickey met the youngest daughter, Phyllis, who was an accountant in London and had her own business advising people on their finances and preparing income taxes. Mickey fell in love with her and after the funeral she asked him to bring her with him to Tobago.

When they had gone to see Uncle Timothy, Uncle Timothy was so glad to see them, he blurted out, "Finally, it seems as though yuh intend to settle down, and give yuh parents some grandpickney." He turned to Phyllis and said, "Nuh mak heh get way yuh nuh; yuh nuh know how long meh bin ah sen and tell dat boy fuh married to one ah dem Yankee women, and give heh father som Yankee gra-pickney." The couple had a pleasant time in Tobago, where Mickey introduced her to those of his childhood friends who were still at home; they went to the beach and passed by Grandie River.

Mickey was surprised to see that the swamp had dried up and that grass was growing where the swamp used to be. On a hill besides the swamp, and where the doctor, who Mickey had met when the doctor was a patient at the hospital during Mickey's early days in America, and who had shown Mickey an artificial waterfall on a model of a resort he was planning to build when he had retired, were some grown grape trees; a neighboring estate had been parceled up and sold. Mickey didn't know what had become of that doctor; but, he never did return to Tobago to build his dream casino. The adjacent area had become a new village and sediments during the construction of new homes and a large playing field had been washed into the tributaries that fed the swamp, and filled up one of one of the tributaries completely. Mickey passed by an area where he and his friends used to go to look for some stunted crabs with big fins to be used as baits, whenever they went to fish on the rocks by the sea when he was growing up. He remembered that they would often come upon oil and lumps of tar, and they wondered from where they were coming. Mickey inspected the area more carefully, and noticed that the vegetation in that area seemed to be somewhat stressed. Before he left Tobago, he heard that the Government had discovered oil off the coast of Tobago, were surveying the coast, and had put out bids to the public. He retuned to Grandie River and took some soil samples of the stressed area, and planned to take them back to his laboratory for analysis of hydrocarbons. He suspected that where Grandie River used to be was on top of a field of oil, and planned to acquire the property.

After they had left Trinidad and Tobago and gone back to England and the United States, they spent many hours talking long-distance over the telephone to each other. A little more than a year later they sent to tell their parents that they coming home to marry each other, and wanted to have a reception at the *great house.* Mickey sent to tell Henry Scott that he wanted him to be his *best-man.* That was another occasion for the families to get together. Henry took along his wife and children; except Rookmine, who didn't care for the wedding, all of Mr. Ramdeen's children and other relatives were in attendance; Mickey's family and some of his childhood friends were there. Mr. Ramdeen had gone up to Tobago several days before the wedding and he was able to show his grandchildren the house that he used to live in when he was a watchman; also, the spot by the river where he had found the chest of gold. Paul's son was on vacation from the United States navy and he had gone to Tobago to see his mother's parents. During the wedding reception someone told Paul that the youth had come home and Paul went to pick him up in order to bring him to meet the rest of his family; at that time Paul and the young man's mother had broken off their relationship. Mickey and Phyllis were holding their wedding reception outdoors on the lawn of the *great house,* when it began to rain. They moved indoors to a banquet hull in an upper story of the house. However, the children were playing in a lobby on a lower portion of the house, next to a car port. Suddenly, there was a crack of thunder, and Henry's last child ran upstairs hollering. Paul's son and one of the other grown-ups were coming to his aid and when they met, the little boy sprang in Paul son's arms and buried his face in the son's bosom.

One of the older people exclaimed, "Heh smell heh family blood; ieh didn't tek long fuh dem to know one another."

Sandra Scott-Ramdeen and her children had moved into a portion of the *great-house* after her husband had drowned, and she would arrange for the rental of the remaining portion. Besides being able to keep the *great house* and the landscape business, the Scott's siblings were able to hold on to the building at the former *pay-yard* and the surrounding lands. Paul had begun to farm some sheep for which he had retained Mr. Stanley Willis to handle. Miss Ellen and Amman were still working at the *great-house* and when there was much work to be done Mr. Stanley Willis would assist them. There was no more need for the book-keeper as all of the other workers were laid off. Paul would drive some the heavy equipment himself to do any landscaping job they got; and, when there was much work to be done, he would hire some extra help.

At first, Mickey returned to the United States by himself, while his wife went back to England. However, they began to seek immediately a U.S. visa for her to join him. When she was eventually allowed in the U.S., she went back to school to do advanced study in Accounting. She become a certified public account, and went to work for a firm on Wall Street in New York City, New York. Mickey was negotiating to buy the lands around where Grandie River used to be; he had found the soil samples he had brought back to the laboratory to have a very high hydrocarbon content.

CHAPTER SEVEN

We Can Make It Together

PHYLLIS RE-ENROLLED IN A college right after she came to the U.S. to do a Master's degree in Accounting, and while at the same time she studied to take her CPA examination. They rented an apartment in Brooklyn, New York where there was a large West Indian community. Life for them was very hectic, but they were determined to make it together. Mickey showed her where to catch her various trains to get to school and work. He had a car, but he was working in New Jersey, and had to leave home at an early hour in the morning to beat the traffic. He had been systematically saving same money to purchase the property at Grandie River, and when he had sufficient to make a down payment, he wrote his father to say that he was coming home on a vacation, and that he planned to do some transaction while he was there.

Phyllis was a very smart person and she completed her Master's degree and took her CPA examination after only two years. At first, she had begun to work as a receptionist for a firm on Wall Street that was offering tuition reimbursement to its employees that were going to school and taking job-related courses. Then she got a promotion to the Accounting Department, and was privy to various investments. She saw that the price of oil was rising phenomenally and, knew that her husband was interested in entering the oil market; but, she had mixed feelings about him leaving his job at the laboratory to go into his own business, which had no guaranteed outcome.

Mickey was keeping Henry Scott and his brother-in- law, the architect, aware of his plans, and suggested to them that they should form a company to search for oil in the swamp at Grandie River. While he was at work he ran into a young engineer, with whom he had taken some classes at college. The engineer had just returned from Alaska where he and another young entrepreneur had gone searching for oil. They had bought a set of expensive computerized equipment and lost much of it underground. When they had run out of money, there was a disagreement between them, and they dissolved the venture. The engineer was then working on his own in New Jersey where he was able to find plenty of environmental work. Many cities had several abandoned factories with leaking underground chemical tanks which had contaminated the immediate properties and adjacent ones. These areas were known 'brown fields' and the State government wanted them cleaned up, sold off and put back on the tax-roll. Using the skills and the know-how which he had acquired in Alaska, the engineer was able to drill various horizontal wells beneath those abandoned factories, in order to vacuum out the contaminants. He was very successful in his work, and had said that he was looking forward to retire at a young age. As Mickey listened to his success story, he became quite anxious to go home to Trinidad and Tobago and to start exploring for oil at Grandie River. He and Phyllis had discussed the matter over and over again; she thought the risk was too much: both she and Mickey had good paying jobs. Henry and his wife were living quite comfortably and Henry didn't want to put her through moving again. Despite Henry's advice that Mickey shouldn't quit his job; and resistance from his wife, Mickey thought that it wouldn't hurt to buy the property at Grandie River.

Mickey and his wife both had jobs which allowed them to carry over one week's vacation from one year to another, so they came home to Trinidad and Tobago together. At that time Phyllis's older sister, Mina, had returned from England to Trinidad where she was practicing law. Therefore, they hired her to do the legal work in acquiring the property that Mickey wanted to buy. The Government was still doing an environmental assessment of those areas, where it had surveyed for oil, before it would allow any oil exploration. After five weeks off from hard work and they have had some rest and relaxation, Mickey and Phyllis returned to New York. They had just gone back to work when Phyllis was determined to be pregnant. However, there was a retired nurse from Trinidad who lived next door, and she was of great assistance to Phyllis during her pregnancy. Phyllis returned to work shortly after the baby was born, and Mickey would get up early to help her get the baby ready to be brought to the next door neighbor. The baby was only ten months old when Phyllis was pregnant again. When Mickey's mother heard about it, she called her sister who was living in Canada with one of her two sons who had sponsored her to that country. Mickey and Phyllis bought a bigger house on Long Island, New York, in anticipation of their growing family, and the aunt from Canada came down to help them move into their Long Island home.

Just about the some time, the company for which Mickey was working announced that it was moving to one of the southern states in the U.S., and offered its employees retraining to get work elsewhere, and continue to pay their salaries, a week's salary for every year they were with the company, up to a full year's salary in payments; or until the employees found other work. At the same time, some fishermen in Tobago were protesting that their livelihood would be at risk, if the Government allowed any oil exploration near the sea; this was holding up the environmental assessments of the various proposals. Mickey was following the developments in Tobago closely on the internet, and he would often say to himself: *Plans delayed don't have to be plans completely denied; if I can't explore for oil, at least I would own a piece of land in Tobago, to which I can look forward to retire, and to leave for my children.*

His aunt from Canada stayed with them a full six-month before she returned to Canada. By that time Phyllis had the second baby; they then had two sons, named Raja and Alex, and after the aunt had left, Mickey would baby sit, while Phyllis went back to work. One day Mickey got a call from his civil engineer friend, who had been doing environmental remediation work in New Jersey. The engineer said that a laboratory, that had been doing analysis for him, was up for sale; and he would buy it, if Mickey would agree to manage it for him. Mickey's continuing monthly salaries were running out, but he didn't want to go back to work for anyone; therefore, he told the engineer that if he could stall the acquisition of the laboratory until Mickey's continuing salaries had ran out, he only would agree to manage the laboratory, provided he become a full partner in the acquisition.

The engineer agreed and when Mickey was ready to go back to work, Mickey and his wife had made arrangements for him to bring their boys to the nurse in Brooklyn who used to assist them, before he went to work at the laboratory they had just purchased, and which was located in Staten Island, New York. He and Phyllis pooled their resources together, but they were under much strain: they had a mortgage on their new home; they were making payments on the property at Grandie River; moreover, he had to meet his share of the expenses of in operating the newly acquired laboratory. However, it is said that *behind every good man is a good woman*. Mickey admitted that without Phyllis at his side, he wouldn't make it: They deprived themselves of vacations and weekend parties that were held by their friends. They would forego eating out, and Phyllis would rather cook at home. They were extremely frugal with their finances, and reminded themselves that they were sacrificing on account of their sons' future well-being. Mickey would put in many long hours in the laboratory, before picking up his sons from the babysitter's in Brooklyn at night. Sometimes he would get home when his wife had prepared dinner and was already in bed. However, she would get up to talk to Mickey and the boys while they were eating, and before they finally turned in to bed for the night.

The laboratory had a large clientele, and customers would come from both New York and New Jersey. Although Mickey had hired a few of technicians that used to work for the former owners of the laboratory, at times he had to perform some analyses himself to prevent a backlog on any report. After a while he found it necessary to hire someone to solicit future customers, and to pick up samples from additional customers in order to compete with other laboratories that performed the same work. Often the person seeking new customers would call up various laboratories to see how much they would charge to do a certain analysis; and, where practical, Mickey would try to beat the competitor's prices. Some technicians who used to work under Mickey at the precious metal refinery, where he used to work before, began to call him up, desiring to work at his current laboratory and he was able to hire some of them.

As time passed by, Phyllis began to handle the accounting and the payroll of the current laboratory. Mickey took the time-cards and other paper-works home, and his wife would handle the pay-checks and other accounts. One day Mickey heard that his former employer was taking bids to remediate the property on which the refinery had sat. There were thirty-five separate buildings which occupied a piece of land of approximately fifty acres, and most of the buildings were heavily contaminated with asbestos and other chemicals. Mickey encouraged his partner to put in a bid. He was quite familiar with all the buildings, and knew what operation went on in each of them. The engineer didn't place the lowest one, but he won the bid; and, sent various samples during the environmental clean up to Mickey's laboratory for analysis. It was a big account, and, at one point, Mickey had to hire extra technicians. There were days when he had gone into the field to supervise taking some samples. The project lasted more than two years, and when it was over, Mickey decided to take a vacation. Uncle Timothy was very anxious to see his "Dougla nephews", and Mickey decided to take the boys along to meet both sides of their relatives. When they landed in Trinidad and Tobago, Mr. Ramdeen was at the airport to meet them. Mickey first went to Arima where he visited various members of the Ramdeen's family. Also, he visited the Carib settlement, which he always did whenever he was in Trinidad. When he returned to Port of Spain he took the boys to see Mr. Ossie's cousins in St. James, before they finally flew on to Tobago. His parents and Uncle Timothy had prepared a big Welcome Home party for them. Uncle Timothy seemed to take possession of the boys: he didn't want to put them down. Paul was in attendance, and he was still keeping away from drugs. He had remained in the landscape business and his flock of sheep had grown into well over five hundred heads, and Mr. Stanley Willis was taking care of them. Miss Ellen and Amman were still around. Mickey brought the boys to the *great house* where they met Mrs. Sandra Scott-Ramdeen and her children.

The next day they went to the beach, and they passed by Grandie River. Uncle Timothy was raising pigs on the property, and the boys were very scared of them. Mickey and the boys spent a wonderful two weeks in Tobago. A week before they went back to America, Suzanne, one of Mickey's cousins, had an appointment with the U.S. Embassy in Port of Spain to seek a student's visa in order to attend a school in New York where she planned to enroll in a Computer Programming program. Mickey accompanied her to the Embassy to get the visa. While they were returning to where they were staying in Port of Spain, and, as they were walking down Frederick Street they came upon Mickey's old f lame at high school. She had returned to Trinidad several years before, after being expelled from Canada for taking a leading role in a Caribbean students' protest over alleged unfair discrimination by her school. She was then caring of her sick mother in Trinidad; her older sister had completed her Ph. D. and was teaching in Canada; her older brother was an executive in a firm in Trinidad, and her younger brother had died of a drug overdose in one of prisons.

Mickey and his cousin went back to Tobago in the evening, and they planned to fly out to Miami two days later. One of Mr. Ramdeen's daughters, Rookmine, that had been managing his Tobago jewelry store at Scarborough went to Mickey's parents' house to see her little nephews before they went back to America, and she brought each of them a gold ring from the store. When they landed in Miami, her brother Sonny, the architect, who had gone to school there and had married an American woman, was on vacation at his in-laws', and he came to airport to see his nephews. He took them all out to lunch before they boarded a f light for Newark, New Jersey. They arrived home way passed mid-night because, through some mix-up, the airline had misplaced their luggage in Miami.

Mickey and his wife had agreed to provide the cousin room and board; and, in return, she would assist them in caring for the boys. Phyllis accompanied the cousin to her school during the first few days, before Phyllis went to work at Wall Street. The cousin had signed up for some classes in the mornings and for others in the evenings, where-ever sessions were offered. She quickly learned the New York transportation system. Mickey and Phyllis thought her to be alert and to observe what was going around her at all times; avoid strangers and to be aware of where the nearest policeman was; they always prayed for her safety. Mickey took the lead, and he sought a local church for his family and attended services regularly. Although his wife wasn't brought up in a Christian church, she didn't oppose when he suggested that they join a Baptist church that was in their neighborhood. When a young minister had gone looking for children to enroll in his church's vacation Bible school, they enrolled their two sons, and thought that it was a good opportunity for Mickey's cousin to help out at the vacation Bible school and to meet other young people. One summer the civil engineer and Mickey agreed to hold a joint picnic for all their employees and their relatives. Charles, a nephew of the engineer, met Mickey's cousin Suzanne: they were both in college, and pursuing Computer Programming. Moreover, their schools were located not too far from each other's. They soon seemed to be inseparable at the picnic. A few weeks later Charles showed up at Mickey's house to accompany Suzanne to church.

Two years had gone by, and an anonymous person had offered a scholarship to any foreign student who had maintained a 3.5 grade point average and above in their studies for the first two years in school. Suzanne had achieved a 4.0 the first year and a 3.6 the second. When she called her aunt in Canada to tell her that she had won a scholarship, her cousin, the computer programmer, offered to send her a round-trip ticket to go home to Tobago for Christmas. Charles her boyfriend, the civil engineer's nephew, wanted to travel to the Caribbean with her. She stayed at her parent's, while he stayed at a local boarding house. This was another mixed-race relationship, and Mr. Ossie and Uncle Timothy were sure to let the young man meet Paul and Mrs. Sandra Scott-Ramdeen. One day Paul had taken him for a ride into Scarborough, and he went into Ramdeen's Jewelry Store to purchase an engagement ring. On their way back to America, and while their plane was in the sky, Charles asked Suzanne if she would marry him, and she said yes.

When they went back to school, every day he would pick her up in the morning and bring her home in the evening. He was one year ahead of her in class, and when he graduated from college, he assisted his uncle in doing environmental work. They soon decided to get marry in a civil ceremony, and two of their friends from school were their witnesses. She proceeded to file for her *"green card"*. They had kept the marriage a secret from their families; he continued to live at home, and she at Mickey and Phyllis'. The *"green card"* application had successfully gone through, but she had to leave the country in order to receive it. The niece and her husband both went to Canada to receive the *green card,* and when her aunt discovered that they had gotten married only in a civil ceremony the aunt wanted them to have a church wedding. The aunt began to plan a date, and wanted them to get marry in Canada. She made arrangements for the bride's mother, Mickey's mother and a few other relatives from Tobago to come to Canada for the wedding. Mickey and Phyllis and their boys drove up to Canada, and so did the civil engineer and other invited relatives of his.

Suzanne and her newly-wedded husband waited until she had graduated from college before they moved into a small apartment not too far away from Mickey and Phyllis' home; that way she was still able to lend a hand in babysitting the children. The niece's husband had got a job providing computer security for a large Inter-net company, and when his wife had graduated from college, he assisted her in getting a job in the same company. Mickey's sons were then in nursery school, and his niece and her husband would get off work before Mickey or his wife; therefore, Suzanne would pick up the boys, take them home and make dinner for both families. She continued to do most of the things she used to do at Mickey's home before she got married. When it was time for them to go bed, she and her husband would go home to their apartment. On weekends the little boys spent much time with her and her husband at their home after church; they adored her husband and loved the places he would take them. About six months after she was married the niece became pregnant, and one day when she was about five months into the pregnancy, she tried to push a heavy desk at work and hurt herself. That night she noticed that she was bleeding slightly; she called her gynecologist to report what had happened and she was given an appointment to come into the doctor's office the next day. After the doctor had examined the niece, she asked to speak to Charles, and they were told that nothing could be done to save the pregnancy; they were devastated, and Charles seemed to be beside himself.

Suzanne was sent to a hospital to prepare for a procedure to remove the remains of the fetus. Phyllis stayed with them for a short time after the niece had been discharged from the hospital. The little boys were told that the niece had lost her unborn baby, and they too shared in the lost of their unborn cousin.

CHAPTER EIGHT

The Scott Family Reunion

PAUL SCOTT HAD NOT been to London since his mother's funeral, and Henry had not been home to Tobago since he attended Mickey's wedding. Paul had gone from being an irresponsible youth addicted to drugs to a mature man that had become addicted to hard work. He spent many long hours behind the wheels of some heavy landscape equipment. He had two assistants, George and Joseph; and sometimes Mr. Stanley Willis would pitch in. In fact, he and Mr. Stanley Willis would make time each day to speak to each other; he had really come to like Mr. Stanley Willis who was like a father to him. Paul's sister, Sandra, was the one who had suggested that they hold a family reunion in London. Miss Ellen and Mr. Amman had been with them for a very time and Sandra and Paul felt that they could entrust them with running their affairs in Tobago while they were gone. Mr. Stanley Willis, although he didn't "know books" would come up at times with some very bright ideas; so, the Scott's siblings had said that he should consulted on any major decision while they were gone.

Sandra had a son and a daughter, and Henry had two boys and a girl just as their parents did. Paul never got married, but he had a son, with whom he'd been keeping in touch and who was in his last year in college, after leaving the U.S. navy. The youth was in college paid for by his Government Issue (G.I.) bill. He seemed to have had a natural gift for fixing things and was studying to become a mechanical engineer. Paul wanted him to be at the family reunion, and he agreed to meet his father in London, where they would stay in the same hotel and go to the reunion together. His father planned to be in London for only a month, since his son had to get back to America to enroll for his final year at college. Paul's sister, Sandra, had planned to stay a little longer. She had many old friends with whom she had gone to school, and wanted to catch up with them. George drove Paul and Sandra's family to the airport, and Miss Ellen, Mr. Amman, and Mr. Stanley Willis went along for the ride. Mr. Stanley Willis was very annoyed to hear George addressing the Scotts as Sandra and Paul to their faces on the way. He wanted George to address Paul as "Sa" or "Misa" and Sandra, as "Ma'am" or "Miz"; he said that George lacked some "manners" toward his employers. When Sandra and Paul objected, he insisted; he thought it was only being respectful. When they got to the airport he didn't want Sandra to move any luggage; he said that if her father were alive, he never would've allowed her to tote her luggage; moreover, he said that the main reason he had come along for the trip was to carry their luggage.

When Paul and Sandra arrived at their hotel in London, Paul's son, whose name was Phillip, had gotten there ahead of them, and already checked into a hotel which Henry had booked for them to stay. Henry and his family, although they lived in the City, were not going to be staying in their home for a week, but had booked rooms in the same hotel for the duration of that time. Henry's children and Phillip quickly got reacquainted, and his youngest child, William, seemed to have staked out an ownership of Phillip: William would not let his older siblings, Myron and Elizabeth, have an opportunity to be alone with Phillip. Phillip and Henry's children had gone out in the City, when Paul, Sandra and her children, Violet and Stephen, arrived by taxi. Paul, Sandra, Henry and his wife Margaret were lingering in the hotel's lobby, while Stephen and Violet were looking at some other children swimming in a pool, when Phillip and his others cousins returned to the hotel from their brief tour of the City.

Sandra had planned a schedule of the events that they were going to follow while they were in London. The day after their arrival, everyone was free to do as he/she pleased, but the next day they planned to visit their mother's grave in the morning and clean it up in preparation for a grave-side ceremony the following Sunday. In the evening they would go to Buckingham Palace to see the changing of the guards before going out to dinner. The next day was a Saturday, and after meeting with a priest whom they wanted to conduct a special service for their family, they would visit other relatives in London. On Sunday after the church service, they proceeded to the cemetery where the priest conducted the special ceremony over their mother's grave. From there they went to their aunt's (the senior Mr. Scott's only surviving sister) home where they had a cook-out with other relatives of the Scott's family.

Mr. Scott's brother in London had died a couple of years before, and his sister, her children and his children then owned the jewelry store. They visited the jewelry store the next day, Monday, before going to see another store which Sandra used to manage on behalf of mother; the new proprietor was then dealing in haberdasheries. Paul wanted to buy a suit in London which he had promised Mr. Stanley Willis to bring back for him; and the whole family helped him to pick one out. Sandra couldn't make up her mind concerning what to buy for Miss Ellen and Amman. They didn't specify any thing in particular, but Sandra knew that she couldn't let Paul take back a suit for Mr. Stanley Willis, and she didn't take something's worthy for them. Violet saw a beautiful pink dress that she thought Miss Ellen would like, and her cousin Elizabeth agreed. The two girls pressured Sandra to buy the dress. Sandra didn't want to buy another suit for Mr. Amman, as she knew that Mr. Stanley Willis would compare it to his suit.

Henry's wife told her that there was no rush because there was plenty of time for them to come up with something. Stephen asked, "What about George and Joseph? Uncle Paul, you have to buy something for them, too." As they proceeded to window shop, they kept an open eye for some suitable gifts. They had lunch at a fancy restaurant before they continued to sight-see. When they returned to their hotel, they were all tired, and went to rest up. Then next day, in the late morning, Sandra, Henry and Violet went to look up one of Sandra's old friend from school. Paul had already taken the other children for a walk around the City. As they were passing an electronic store, the children wanted go inside. Myron said, "Uncle Paul, I know what you can buy." He went across the isle and picked up a portable radio. On a shelf right next to the radio was a tape recorder, and Stephen said, "Uncle Paul, you can buy both of them as gifts." Paul *thought, he could buy the portable radio for George, and the tape recorder for Joseph, who thought of himself as an aspiring calypsonian, to record and listen to the ballads he used to sing,* Paul made the purchases, and Phillip saw an electrical guitar which he bought for himself. After leaving that store they went to another store where Phillip bought a deep-fry pot that ran on electric for his mother. They returned to their hotel to leave their purchases before they went in search of the other adults. They caught up with them at Henry and his siblings' aunt's home, where they spent the evening well into the late hours, speaking about old times before they returned to their hotel to spend the night. When a week was up and it was time for Henry and his family to check out of the hotel, the whole clan accompanied them home. Henry and Margeret had planned a cook-out, and the young people had more fun together. Although that wasn't planned, Elizabeth and Violet wanted to spend the night together, so Stephen and Myron decided that they should spend the night together, too. However, William decided that he wanted to go back to the hotel to be with Phillip. Myron and Elizabeth wanted to take Stephen and Violet to school with them the next day, and their parents didn't object.

During their stay in London, Paul had an opportunity to visit some of his past hung-outs. Some of his former buddies were still around, and although some of them were married and had children, they were still smoking marijuana, and were surprised when Paul told them that he had *"kicked the habit":* he was then *"clean";* he didn't want to have anything to do *"with that stuff any more, and hoped that none of his younger relatives would start to do that foolishness."* A month went by much too quickly for the children, and soon it was time for Paul's to go home to Tobago, and Phillip to America. William was heart-broken; he didn't seem to understand why he couldn't go to America, too, and stay with Cousin Phillip. The day before Paul and Phillip left England, Sandra wanted the entire clan to meet at their mother's grave once more to pay their final respects to the deceased. She had bought some religious relics, a picture of their mother, and had a new one of the entire family that she wanted to leave of her mother's grave.

Before their two-months were up, Henry and Margeret suggested to Sandra that she and her children should check out of their hotel and come and stay with them. Sandra could sleep with the girls, while Stephen, Myron and William would occupy Myron and William's room. Everyone liked the idea; that way Sandra could prepare meals for everyone while Henry and Elizabeth had gone to work. The children especially enjoyed the arrangement, and they were up late into the night talking many things that all children loved to talk about, and asking many questions about their family's history. When it was time for Sandra and her children to leave London, they had planned to travel very late in the evening, but their f light was delayed, and they left in the wee hours of the morning. They arrived at Piarco Airport, Trinidad after a long trans-Atlantic f light and caught a connecting f light Crown Point, Tobago. Paul was there with Mr. Stanley Willis to meet them. Mr. Stanley Willis was wearing his gift suit, which he had already worn several times since Paul had given it to him: he had worn it to church and into town when he accompanied Paul to shop. He had said that the suit made him feel respectable, and that people would respect you according to how you dress.

When they arrived back at the *great house* Miss Ellen thank Sandra for her new dress, which she planned to wear only on special occasions: such as a village harvest, or if someone had invited her to a wedding. Mr. Amman was living at the side of the mansion, in a little building, and a wing of the *great house* was blocking a breeze from the sea. On sunny days, the little building became quite hot and uncomfortable. Therefore, he installed his fan in one of the windows and it was working constantly. Each passenger was only allowed to carry a limited of weight on the airplane; therefore, Paul had left behind George and Joseph's gifts for Sandra and her children to bring. They treasured both gifts, but while George would bring his radio to work, Joseph played his tape recorder only at home. Sandra had bought a relic to lie on their father's grave, and she had a copy of a picture of the entire family which she wanted to put beside a picture of him. Miss Ellen, Amman and Mr. Stanley Willis went along with them to Sir John Salvi's Cemetery where he was buried. Mr. Stanley Willis and Paul had gone a few days before to clean up the surroundings of the grave. They brought along an Anglican priest from St. Mary's district to perform a ceremony and to pray for the deceased. Miss Ellen had the first opportunity to wear her pink dress in public. Mr. Stanley Willis stood at attention beside her after the ceremony, and wanted Paul to take a picture of them.

While they were in London, Sandra, Henry and Margaret had discussed the feasibility of Sandra sending back her children to London to go to school; however, they deferred on the timing and thought it was better to wait until the children had finished high school in Tobago. There was a prestigious high school in Tobago, and if one had the proper connection, one could get one's children to go there, or to one of the elite high schools in Trinidad. Sandra had known some upper class people, some of her father's friends, who recommended that her children be accepted into the high school in Tobago. On evenings after school they would get a ride from a large property owner into the town proper, where they would go to help out their aunt in the branch of Ramdeen's Jewelry Store at Scarborough, until Uncle Paul or George came to pick them up and bring them home to the great house.

During vacation from school Stephen started to hang out with his uncle Paul, Mr. Stanley Willis, George and Joseph. He would often go with Mr. Stanley Willis to look after his fish traps in the river for he had heard about Mr. Stanley Willis' discovery of the chest of gold several years ago. His grandfather, Mr. Ramdeen, had also told him that he had found one chest, too, and according to what he understood, one chest was still missing; Stephen hoped that he would find it. The adults had told him about the dangers of alligators and some evil mysteries in the river. Mr. Stanley Willis had given him a fetish to hang around his neck whenever he was in the vicinity of the river. When Sandra had told her father- in- law about the boy's interest in finding the missing chest of gold, he brought the boy some of his own fetishes when he had come to Tobago to see how his daughter was managing his Tobago store. After every rainfall and when the river had subsided, the boy would go looking along the banks of the river by himself. His mother had become quite concerned and told him that if he wouldn't stop, she was going to send him to Trinidad to live with his dad's father. Mr. Ramdeen would be delighted to have him: he had told

Sandra that he had sufficient connections to get the boy into one of the prestigious high school in Trinidad. However, the boy didn't want to live in Trinidad, and promised his mother that he wouldn't go searching by himself again, and except his uncle Paul or Mr. Stanley Willis was with him.

Stephen completed high school in Tobago and took the Senior Cambridge School Leaving Certificate examination. He did very well in the tests, and his mother wanted him to complete his education in London. Her husband had provided very well for his family in the event something should happen to him -- he had left several thousand dollars worth of life insurance. Both she and her husband wanted Stephen to follow in his father's foot-steps and become a doctor, too. Therefore, she would send the boy off to London to study premed then he would do *Medicine*. Mr. Ramdeen wanted him to spend sometime in Arima with him and his relatives before he went away to study, and after sitting the school leaving examination and while he was awaiting the results. During that time he went along with one of his cousins who grew lots of vegetables for the Port of Spain market. After the results of his examination had come out, he went up to Tobago before coming back to Trinidad with his mother to go to the American Embassy and the British Consulate to apply for the various document that he would need to travel abroad. Miss Ellen, Mr. Amman, and Mr. Stanley Willis went to Crown Point Airport with the whole family when he was finally leaving Tobago for London. Mr. Stanley Willis hugged the youth and cried like a baby to see him go. His mother, sister and Uncle Paul would accompany him as far as Piarco Airport, Trinidad, where they met with members of the Ramdeen's family. Stephen had planned to visit his aunt Phyllis for a week in New York before going on to London. When he arrived in New York Paul's son who had already graduated from college and was on vacation from his job where he had been working as a mechanical engineer, was at the airport to meet him; all the other family members were either at work or school. Phyllis had scheduled his stay in New York around a week-end so they would have an opportunity to take him around to see various sites in the City before he traveled to London. His cousin Phillip took him to the campus of the college where he had gone to school, and he was awestruck by the various students hustling to their classes. The next day they went to see Uncle Mickey at work in the laboratory, before going on to Wall Street where his aunt Phyllis worked. He went with Suzanne and her husband Charles to work the next day, and much too soon the time was up before he would go on to London and enroll for his classes.

In London he would be staying in a boarding house, which was owned by a family from Trinidad, and which was the same one where Mr. Ramdeen's daughters stayed when they lived in London. The location wasn't very far away from where his uncle Henry lived, and Sandra believed that her son wouldn't get too home-sick with family members so near. Uncle Henry and his family met him at the airport, and two days later, he and his cousins Myron and Elizabeth accompanied Stephen to his college for his registration. He went to see his great aunt in her jewelry store and brought her his mother's deepest regards. His great aunt told hm to call on her at any time he found himself in need. Myron and Elizabeth wanted to spend more time with him, but their father told them to give him some privacy to write to his mother and all the folks back in Trinidad and Tobago; and to do whatever he had to take care of. There would be much time afterwards for them to get together.

CHAPTER NINE

The Ramdeen Family Reunion

M R. RAMDEEN HAD TWO boys and three girls: the oldest, Sonny, was an architect who had studied in Florida and married to Emily an American White woman; the second child was Mina who had obtained a law degree in the United Kingdom before retuning to Trinidad and married to Sookdeo, her childhood sweetheart of Indian descent; the third was Kumar, who had studied *medicine* both in Canada and the U.K. before returning home to work for the Trinidad government. He was married to Sandra Scott and had drowned off the coast of Tobago one weekend when he had gone spear-fishing; the fourth child was Rookmine who had gone to England to study Law, but after a year and a half, she couldn't really decide what she wanted to do; so, she asked her father to bring her home to help him manage his jewelry stores. She got married to Nandi another Trinidadian of East Indian descent. And, the fifth and last child was Phyllis, an accountant, who had married Mickey Orr and they had two sons Raja and Alex.

Ever since they had heard of the Scott's reunion, the Ramdeens wanted to have a reunion of their own. Their parents were getting up in age, and they had not all been together since Kumar's funeral. When Phyllis and Mickey had gotten married Rookmine and her husband didn't attend the wedding because they didn't want it to happen. However, they had since been reconciled, and they had seen Phyllis' children for the first time when Mr. Ramdeen had brought the boys to their home. Also, when they were in Tobago on vacation, Rookmine had gone to see them once. The Ramdeens planned the reunion for when all their children and grand children, who were in school, were out on summer break. Sonny had a son named Fred, who was then enrolled in the same architectural school to which his father had gone in Florida; and, a daughter, Dolly, who had gone off to Jamaica on a Trinidad and Tobago Government scholarship to study *Economics.* As for Mina: she had a boy, Kumar, and two girls, Eudaris and Iris. Besides her private law practice, Mina was also an adjunct professor of law at a university in Trinidad, and she helped Kumar and Eudaris, the older girl, to get scholarships to attend that school to study *Law.* The younger girl Iris after finishing high school, didn't want to go to college; so, she helped her grand-parents in managing the jewelry store in Port of Spain; The late Dr. Kumar was the father of Stephen (Scott-Ramdeen) who was then in his third year as a premed student in London, and Mr. Ramdeen urged his mother to bring him home for the occasion. His sister Violet was still in high school in Tobago; Rookmine had only one daughter, Mona, who also didn't want to go to college after she had finished high school; but, instead, to help manage all the jewelry stores; she traveled among the stores in Arima, Port of Spain and Tobago; Phyllis, Mickey and their two boys, Roja and Alex, would be coming from New York for the occasion.

They wanted to have a picnic for the whole family at the reunion, and they chose for the venue, a beach not far away from Scarborough, Tobago and from where Dr. Kumar had gone to sea when he drowned. They reserved a few guest houses in Tobago where all the family would stay, and a restaurant owner, Mrs. Ramnarine, would be catering East Indian and other Trinidad foods during the picnic. In addition to the family cars, they hired a maxi-taxi from Trinidad to be on stand-by to take the whole family around to various places which they had planned to visit in Tobago. At eight o'clock in the morning after prayers, they assembled at a shopping mall in Scarborough. The Tobago branch on the Ramdeen's Jewelry Store had been recently relocated to that mall where all the stores were new and there was a large movie house. Mr. Ramdeen wanted everyone to see his new jewelry store and he had several custom-made bracelets on which he had inscribed *The Ramdeen's Family First Reunion;* more than enough for each member of the family to have one, and which should be worn as a memorabilia of the occasion and to ward off any evil influence that might try to do them harm. He had taken the bracelets to be blessed by a Hindu priestess before leaving Trinidad, and insisted that each person wear one. He wanted to show the whole family where he used to live as a watchman, and the spot where he had found the chest of gold; it was there the family's fortune begun. The Scott's *great house* wasn't very far away; but, they went straight to the beach where they had planned to picnic, because Sandra had promised to host a dinner for them at *the great house* the next evening. Mr. Ramdeen had brought along three bottles of incense which he poured along the beach and in the water before anyone had gotten into it. It was an ideal day to be at the beech: the tide was low, and the water had receded towards the ocean, leaving a vast expanse of sand along the seashore. They had organized a beach volley ball game, and also, a soccer game in which they wanted everyone to participate. And, all of them, except the matriarch of the family, whom everyone called Nana, were willing to corporate.

Mina and her mother had gone up to Tobago to join Rookmine when they went to see Mrs. Ramnarine to plan the menu for the event. Although their parents were strict vegetarians, not all of their off-springs were; and whereas they had ordered some vegetarian dishes, most dishes were designed to add meats if anyone wanted. They ordered an abundance of: samosas, chutneys, (mongo, tamarind, mint), saag paneer, pakara/bhaji, landoori, roti, chicken tandoori and tikka musala, chicken vindaloo and chicken korma, chicken jalfrezi, rice kheer, mango lassi, masala chai, and non-alcoholic beverages. Nana and Rookmine went around with Mrs. Ramnarine to make sure they had gotten everything they had ordered. Mrs. Ramnarine had gone ahead of them with extra help to set up various tables and chairs where the food would be served and Nana wanted to see that everything was according to her likeness. She felt that games were for the children and remained in the food area to supervise the distribution. When everyone had gotten out of the vehicles, all gathered together for prayers and remarks from various family members, before they separated into cliques or went into the water. After they had grown tired of playing volley ball and soccer, the younger ones swam in the sea, as they talked to one another about their various classes and the places where they went to school; while the older members lay in the sand and soaked up the rays of the sun.

It was nightfall when they had gotten back to the shopping mall, and they had planned the take in a movie at the new cinema before they retired; however, as some of the older adults were too exhausted, they reconsidered that item on their schedule to be optional, and some went right away to their guest-houses, while the others went to see the movie. Everyone was allowed to sleep late the next day, if they wanted to; but, a cricket match was planned to start at noon at a playground they had reserved for that purpose. Sonny and Mina were the two captains and they had tried to pick the opposing teams fairly; therefore, Mina was allowed the first pick, and Sonny the next; Mina the third, Sonny the fourth, and so on. They wanted everyone to play, even Nana, who happened to be the last picked, and found herself on Sonny's team. A paper bag brunch was delivered to the maxi-taxi for everyone. Also, big pots of black tea, green tea and coffee that one could choose according to one's likeness. It was imperative that the match begin on time in order to end at the anticipated hour because in the evening they would be going to Sandra's house for dinner.

The teams consisted of: Mr. Ramdeen (Grandpa), Nana (Grandma) and Uncle Boland (Grandpa's brother), Boysie (maxi-taxi's driver and son of Boland), Silvia (Kumar's girl-friend who worked in the Port of Spain store); Sonny, Emily (Sonny's wife), Fred (their son); Dolly (their daughter); Mina, Nandi (her husband), Kumar (their son who was named after his uncle the doctor) Eudaris and Iris; Sandra (the wife of the late Dr. Kumar who had drowned at sea while spear-fishing.) Stephen (their son), and Violet (their daughter); Rookmine, Sookdeo (her husband), Mona (their daughter); Phyllis, Mickey (her husband), Roja and Alax (their sons). (Note that Mr. Ramdeen's children are underlined while their spouses and children were explained in brackets), The two opposing teams were as follows:

Team A: Mina (captain), Fred, Nandi, Boysie, Grandpa, Uncle Boland, Alex, Phyllis, Mona, Sandra, Iris and Emily.

Team B: Sonny (captain), Mickey, Stephen, Rookmine, Kumar, Violet, Roja, Dolly, Sookdeo, Eudaris, Silvia and Nana.

Team B won the toss; but, they would rather have Team A to bat first. Fred and Nandi were the opening bat's men, and Fred was run out after trying to steal a crucial run. However, he had put up 18 runs and the partnership 23. Boysie and Nandi put up another 8 runs before Boysie was clean bowled Stephen. Nandi was cought by Mickey, bowled by Stephen. Grandpa had scored 26 in which he made two consecutive 4s but when he tried to score a 6, he was caught on the boundary line by Kumar off the bowling of Dolly. Alex came to bat and he and Uncle Boland scored another 30 runs before Uncle Boland was caught by Soodeo off the bowling of Stephen, Mona scored 2 before she was clean bowled by Kumar; Phyllis was out LBW and scored 3 when she came in to bat against Kumar. Mona scored 1 having been clean bowled by Stephen; Sandra scored 3, clean bowled by Udaris, Iris 5 clean bowled by Kumar. Emily was the 12th man and did not have to bat, Alex was not out having scored 2 runs, and the whole side made a grand total of 88 runs. Wickets were taken as follows: Stephen =3, Mickey =3, Mina =2, Eudaris =1 and run out = 1.

When it was Team A turn to bat, Sonny opened with Stephen and together they scored 15 runs before Stephen was clean bowled Fred for 13 runs; Mickey joined Sonny to reach 23 before Mickey was clean bowled by Fred; Rookmine scored 1 before she was bowled Emily; Dolly made 3 before she was caught by the wicket keeper Nandi off the bowling of Fred; Kumar made a quick 10 during which he scored a 6 and a 4 before he was clean bowled by Fred. Violet clean bowled for 0 by Fred, Dolly was stumped out by the wicket keeper Nandi on the next ball for 0, Sookdeo made 6 runs before he was by caught off the bowling of Boysie, Udaris made 5 before she was clean bowled by Fred, the first ball having tipped her bat and traveled all the way to the boundary for 4; Raja made 2 before he was bowled by Emily, Silvia didn't score having been caught LBW by Emily, and the whole side was out 77; Sonny was not out on a score of 27. Although Sonny scored the highest in the game his team lost the match by 11runs. No one was hurt during the game and Nana didn't have to play being her team's 12th man.

There was refreshment in the maxi-taxi for everyone, and they partook, as they recapped the highlights of the game. On each of the opposite ends of the playground were four metal booths, two for males, and the others for females: there they would go to shower themselves before going to Sandra's dinner. Mr. Stanley Willis had gone early that morning to pump water from a nearby river to fill two elevated galvanized water tanks that supplied the showers. However, Sandra, Mina and a few of the ladies would use the showers at the *great house;* therefore, they left immediately after to game, and drove to Sandra's home. Those ladies also wanted to see that everything for the dinner was in order. Miss Ellen had brought in Mr. Stanley Willis' wife to help her cook. Also, Mr. Amman would be there to do whatsoever they called upon him to do, and Paul had asked Mr. Stanley Willis, George and Joseph to be at the *great house* that evening for the occasion.

The menu would consist of cheese wrapped in roasted tomatoes for an appetizer. Young coconut water which was poured into a wooden keg with a spigot, and from which they could replenish a glass tumbler on each table; this would take the place of wines and was served before the main course. There were vegetarian dishes, but Sandra had ordered a whole large kingfish from a friend of Mr. Stanley Willis, and Paul had donated two of his lambs which he had Mr. Stanley Willis to kill for the occasion. Sandra had also ordered lots of roti and other East Indian foods, but she had Miss Ellen to cook big pots of long grain rice, spaghetti and mixed vegetables to be served with the main course. Paul had acquired a taste for some huge broad wheat-f lour dumplings that the men used to make at the steel-pan tent, and he and George made a pot of it. He got Joseph to bring some breadfruits, and after they had roasted them on barn fire in the back yard of the *great house*, they peeled and fried them. Mr. Amman had picked lots of ripe papayas from a field along the road leading to the *great house,* and Miss Ellen puréed some of them which she mixed with milk and other ingredients to make an exotic drink for dessert; she, also, made some home made ice-cream. George had brought along his gift radio, and someone tuned it into a station broadcasting Indian music out of Guyana. The lawn overlooked the ocean and they could see some ocean liners and other vessels in the distant horizon. Also, there were two bays in sight and some local residents were carrying flambeaux and bol-de-fes as they were night-fishing along the rocks bordering the bays.

During and after the dinner, Mr. Stanley Willis had a very long discussion with Mickey. As they sat on the edge of the lawn on two folding chairs which Mr. Stanley Willis had placed there for them to sit, as they were eating, the old man said to Mickey, "Misa Mickey Orr, yuh doe knah haw mach yuh mak meh feel prawd?"

Mickey laughed at the way he was addressed, and the other man said, "Wha' yuh larfin ath? Dat's yuh nam; yuh knoh? Eif yuh war pepel fuh respec yuh, yuh hah tuh leh dem cal yuh buh yuh ful nam, an lok yuh ina yuh eye."

He brushed off his gift suit that Paul had brought back for him from England a few years ago, and as they were staring out above the ocean and looking at a cruse ship sailing by, Mr. Stanley Willis continued their discussion: "Meh nuh hah enby inah meh hart fuh nuh bodie, ber eif nuh binah fuh yuh, nun eof dese ting wulda tak' plac. Eis yuh wheh fus fin deh gol; an yuh fadar an yuh uncle brin dem tuh Engin Town meny yares ahgo; an wen rain beh wash eit way; ah suh meh gat fuh fine deh fus' ches eof gol; and Misa Ramdeem gat fuh fine deh secand wone; hah suh deh cume buh dem raches. Deh Scotts an deh Ramdeens duin wel, an meh glad tuh seh dat deh nuh lef yuh eout. Meh ole an meh nuh beh tek bok, suh meh nuh beh expec mach. Meh hah wone pickney an sheh nuh beh lik schol, tuh. Sheh hardly culd camb sheh hare whan sheh hah sheh fus pickney."

Just then they could see one of the local men fishing on the rocks adjusting the flame of his bol-de-fe which was going out, and Mr. Stanley Willis got a bright idea: "Haw's yuh cusin, Miss Susan Tamas, dat join yuh inah America doin?" He asked.

Mickey told him she had completed college, gotten married and was doing fine. Also, his mother's sister who had migrated to Canada and her two sons, were all doing okay; one of the boys was a police officer and the other a computer programmer.

"Yuh moda sister pickney eis wah policeman ina Caneda? Meh L-o-r-d; whan yuh hah ambishan, yuh could beh anything dat yuh want tuh deh" he added.

He thought for a moment then he continued, "Yuh family should has a reunion, tuh; suh dat dem whea nuh has nuh ambition, woulda be force tuh lok up; ah mean dat dey would becume motivated. Discuss eit wit yuh farda and yuh morda befo' yuh guh back to America; write yuh antie in Canada, an' alyuh plan sume ting as soon as possible. Ieh don't have tuh beh dis year, ber, deh sooneh deh bettah."

They had served a buffet style dinner under a big tent that Paul, Mr. Amman, Mr. Stanley Willis, George and Joseph had set up on the lawn of the great house. After they had feasted, they played cards, draft, chess and other board games well into night. It was the last time Stephen, Fred and Dolly would see one another before they leave the country to return to schools over-seas; Mickey, Phyllis and their sons would be spending a few more days in Tobago at Mickey's parents' home before they returned to New York; and some of the family members who had to go to work in Trinidad the next day had planned to fly out from Crown Point to Piarco Airports later that morning; the rest of the family who lived in Trinidad would catch a ferry from Scarborough to Port of Spain the following evening. Therefore, they said their parting good-byes about 12:30 a.m. and returned to their various guest houses at the conclusion of an enjoyable *get-together*.

CHAPTER TEN

Moments of Reflection

MICKEY SAT ON THE passenger side of the front seat of a vehicle as George was taking him and his family back to his father's house that night. He seemed to be absorbed in a world of his own, and no one tried to converse with him, thinking that it was because he had gone through a long exhausting day and he was tired. However, he was thinking about Mr. Stanley Willis' private remarks to him that his family ought to hold a family, too. His father and mother had an empty nest: his younger brother Selwyn was living with his Uncle Timothy in a wooden house that the brother and Mickey's long time friend Johnny had constructed for Uncle Timothy near the area where Grandie River used to be; his sister Donna was then living with a grocery store owner in the village -- she had moved in with him after her father had put her out of the parents' house when she had become pregnant by the shopkeeper Kenneth, and Kenneth had refused to marry her because he was seeing someone else at the time; Donna went on to have another child for Kenneth, and still being unmarried. Mickey, his wife and two boys occupied two empty bedrooms of the parents' house while they were visiting, and they went quietly to bed, so as not to disturb the parents.

Mickey was up early; he couldn't sleep much. He took his father's poniard and set out for Uncle Timothy's house before the others were up. He didn't use the old road to get there, but passed by a new one that the Government had built towards the beach. He wanted to see the new development. Along the way there was a new playground that was designed for various types of sports, and modern homes which were landscaped with fruit trees had replaced a field of coconut trees and guinea grass. Mickey passed by one end of a beach where some boats were being stored, and as he was walking towards the opposite one to where Grandie River used to be, he was admiring the surface of the translucent sea, over which a gentle breeze blew, causing the water to form small waves that seemed to be pushing back a murky little stream coming from Par Gully, which no longer f lowed into Grandie River, but was emptying into the sea through a channel which was located about the center of the beach. As he was looking at the sea, he saw a shark swimming along the beach, its dorsal fin projecting above the water, resembling the periscope of a submarine, as it moved.

When Mickey arrived at their home, Uncle Timothy and Selwyn were surprised to see him. His uncle was proud to show off the many pigs that he was breeding. Selwyn would help him to pick breadfruits from the neighboring properties, and to collect food wastes from the villagers to feed them. Grandie River no longer existed; it had been filled in by the soil that had eroded from the new constructions. Also, water usage had changed, and the new developments weren't allowed to have opened discharges, but all the residences were then required to have septic tanks. Very little water, except when it rained, was being discharged into Horse River which f lowed into Par Gully before the latter reached Grandie River. The channel through which Horse River used to f low was almost filled in with soil, as were the marshes around where Grandie River used to be.

Mickey had already discussed Donna's situation with his aunt Enid who lived in Canada, and the aunt had requested that Mickey try to sponsor Donna to get to America. It had been fourteen years since he had made an application for a visa for her, and when last he inquired, the United States Consulate had told him that the remaining waiting time for a hearing was approximately eighteen months. That morning he talked it over with Uncle Timothy and Selwyn and they decided to tell Donna that if she would get married, it would be easier for her visa application to go through. Kenneth would then have an incentive to marry her because he too wanted to go to America. They were going to get married in a civil ceremony, and Mickey would update Donna's information with the US Embassy. When the time had come, they got their visas as a family; however, Donna would travel at first by herself; and, the rest of her immediate family would join her afterward.

After speaking to his uncle and brother, Mickey lay on the beach and ref lected on how things used to be: *He thought about the morning many years ago when he first found the gold. Whatever became of the doctor he had met in the hospital who had built a model casino with a waterfall flowing out of the hill beside Grandie River? Did the other man from Dominica ever get married again and had a family as he had done? There were no little crabs then living in the area; there was no more marsh. Although some oil might be beneath the soil that had filled in Grandie River, there was no sign of any in the new surface on which the pigs were running about. The fishermen had succeeded in getting the Government to proceed with caution: anyone who wanted to explore for oil must have the backing of a large insurance company, should anything go wrong; therefore, the few permits that were being issued were to large oil companies that already had a record of good environmental practices. He and Phyllis had met with a certain degree of success in America, and for the time being he would continue to focus on his laboratory, and she accounting.*

Selwyn was busy with his morning chore of feeding the pigs and when he had finished, he sneaked up behind his brother, and disturbed his day-dreaming. Selwyn seemed very contented with how he and his uncle Timothy were raising their pigs. Also, he would make himself available to help out Johnny when the latter had extra carpentry to do. That morning he and Mickey visited their sister to inform her and Kenneth of what they had decided concerning her going to America. All three siblings and Kenneth proceeded to their parents' home to tell them of the plans: Kenneth would turn over the grocery to Selwyn while he and Donna were in America. By then Uncle Timothy had joined them. The news was too much for their mother to keep from writing her sister in Canada to tell her right away. When she told the sister that a church wedding was planned to follow the civil wedding, the sister suggested that they informed all their relatives, and plan to have a family reunion of their own at a reception after the church wedding. Just what Mickey was thinking! By the time the date they had set for the civil wedding arrived, Mickey and his family would already be back in America. When Mickey got home, the first thing that he did was to call his Aunt Enid in Canada and tell her about the wedding arrangement and about the family reunion he was suggesting that they have at the same time. Donna and her family had no set-backs when they had gone to the U.S. Embassy in Port of Spain for an interview to get their visas. As they had planned, Donna would go to the U.S. by herself at first, and within six months the others would follow. They won't be going back to Tobago before the church wedding and family reunion.

When we last heard from Suzanne and Charles, they had just lost their unborn child; now, they were the proud parents of two little girls. The girls were like little sisters to Mickey and Phyllis' boys, and the rest of the relatives out of the country were very anxious to meet them. Suzanne was the daughter of Mickey's mother's brother who still lived in Tobago. When she first came to America by herself, Donna took care of the two boys and two girls, and she slept in the same room with Charles and Suzanne's little girls. Each evening the whole family would gather around Mickey and Phyllis' dining table to have supper which Donna had prepared for all of them. Then at least once a week after dinner they would call Aunt Enid in Canada to talk over any new development within the family, and on Sunday mornings Donna would use a calling card to speak to her husband and children in Tobago. Mickey had fixed up his basement to make accommodation for Donna's family, and when the others had arrived in America, Mickey was able to obtain a job through a friend at a local hospital for Kenneth.

Kenneth was quite popular and lots of people would want to be at his wedding reception after his church wedding. The Orr family was also well known, and they wanted to invite several persons. Knowing that some relatives would be coming from overseas, and they hadn't spent a Tobago Christmas or Carnival for a long time, they thought it best to plan for the church wedding reception/family reunion to coincide with one of these events; they had chosen a date shortly before Carnival, at first; however, after considering that everyone would be preoccupied with the upcoming Carnival and, not wanting to hold it during Lent, they decided on Easter week-end. They extended an invitation to their Shouter Baptist friends from Trinidad, and Uncle Timothy invited Mr. Ossie's cousin from St.James and his family to the occasion. Mr. Ossie would be bringing out a masquerade band, after being absent from the parades for some years. The village steel pan band no longer practiced on his property, and one of the local companies was then sponsoring them. Paul had renewed his in interest in beating the steel pan and his son Phillip would be coming home from America for the Carnival; Mickey invited the both of them to the reception/reunion. Donna and Paul's son's mother, Sherma, used to beat the steel pans together long ago, and Donna had invited her to the wedding; so, Phillip and his mother would be in Tobago around Carnival. It was an occasion for the two women to beat the steel pans and get together after being apart for many years. They both signed up with Mr. Ossie to play music for his masquerade band.

Aunt Enid's sons had not been back to Tobago since they had left the island several years ago. They had both gotten married and started their families in Canada, and they almost couldn't wait to see what's new in Tobago. They planned to spend the Carnival in Trinidad and go to Tobago immediately afterward. Mickey, Phyllis and their boys would be spending the Carnival with the Ramdeens in Arima, but attending the shows at the Queen Park Savannah in Port of Spain on the week-end before the Carnival; after which they would be going to Tobago and staying in one of the hotels; Mickey had extended invitations for the wedding reception/family reunion to members of the Ramdeen's family.

One evening when Paul had gone to steel pan rehearsal, he found Donna and his son's mother, Sherma, showing his son, Phillip, how to play the steel pan. Paul and Phillip's mother had not spoken to each other since they had broken up many years ago. And, at first, it seemed as if neither of of them wanted to renew their relationship. When Paul joined them, his son's mother walked away, and left Paul and Donna to teach Phillip. Even though it appeared as if neither of them had any interest in renewing their old relationship, evening after evening Paul really hoped that at least she would speak to him, and Phillip longed to see his parents speak to each other. On a Saturday night when the band was rehearsing the calypso tunes they planned to play on Carnival Day; some boys had gone to pick pachro and whelks earlier that day and when they had cooked them, they served them with boiled green bananas, some large wheat f lour dumplings and roasted breadfruits, which had become some of Paul's favorite dishes. Paul was disappointed when Phillip said that didn't like pachro and whelks; he didn't even want to taste the food. Paul told him that he, too, didn't like them at first, but that once he had gotten used to them, he had come to love them. Pachro and whelk broths are the equivalent to the Jamaican 'manish water' and they are quite popular among the Tobago youths. Paul coaxed Phillip to take a little of the broths and told him that once he had gotten used to them, he would love them.

Although most people in Trinidad and Tobago observed Lent, the Orr family was busy making plans for their up-coming *wedding reception/family reunion*. It was the dry season in Tobago and they planned to hold the event at a new play-ground that the Government had just constructed outside Belle Garden. During several days in the Lenten season volunteers had set up bamboo tents to shade attendees from the sun. The Orr wanted the ceremony to resemble a real *old time wedding* and they had made several out-door fire places and planned to cook various foods in big pots in the open. Uncle Timothy made two ovens out of 55-gallon drums on which he had planned to roast two pigs. Days leading up to the event, Johnny, Selwyn, George and Joseph would go hunting in the forest for various bush meats and Mr. Stanley Willis would shoot *man-of-war* birds as they f lew pass a hill above Grandie River. They would preserve them at Sandra and Paul's home in a huge ice box that was kept in a little house outside the *great house*. That was going to be the *mother of all wedding reception/family reunion*, and they wished that no one who wanted to have something, couldn't get it. The local fishermen had gone to fish specifically for the occasion, and among the dishes, they were planning to have fish chowder and barbeque tuna.

Phillip loved to hear his father, Mickey and Mr. Stanley Willis discussing the things that used to happen long ago, and one day Mr. Stanley Willis showed him the spot where he had found the chest of gold. When Phillip learnt that a chest of gold was still missing, he wanted them to renew a search for it. However, Mr. Stanley Willis said, "Meh nar war tuh guh trauw dat agan; eif deh gol shaw eup, whosaeber fine eam guh beh deh lucky wone."

Paul and Mickey thought that someone should've found it a long time ago and Mickey told them that his Uncle Timothy, his brother Selwyn and long time friend Johnny, were still keeping an eye opened to look out for it.

Violet had then finished high school, and when June rolled around her mother would be taking her to join her brother Stephen in London to do premed in the same college that Stephen was attending. Both children wanted to follow in the footsteps of their father Kumar Ramdeen. One Saturday morning Violet had gone with her with her Uncle Paul and Mr. Stanley Willis to their sheep pen to select two rams they planned to sell to the Orrs for their up-coming events; and, as Paul and Mr. Stanley Willis were looking over the herd, Violet was soaking her feet in a river near the sheep pen. She was gazing at a pump in a deep part of the river with a screened section from which Mr. Stanley Willis pumping water to fill a large galvanize tank which was about one-half of a mile away by the *great house,* and the ref lection of a nearby cedar tree, when she saw two pigeons sheltering in its branches. She was glad that Mr. Stanley Willis didn't see them because he would shoot them. Uncle Paul had promised to drive her that afternoon by the old hospital and the district medical clinic at which her father used to work when they had first come to Tobago; she wanted to bring back to mind what seemed to be the *good old days* that she and her brother used to have before their father died. Also, she thought of her grandfather, her mother's Sandra's father; she had planned to pass by Sir John Silvi's Cemetery to see his grave once more.

Violet's cousin Phillip and Mr. Stanley Willis would be coming along for the ride. When they had gone to pick up Phillip, the young man had already finally coaxed his mother to come along for the ride. Mr. Stanley Willis was seated in the front, passenger side of the vehicle, wearing the English suit Paul that had given him, while Violet was seating in the back; Phillip and his mother joined her. They viewed the old hospital from the outside before they went up to the top of Fort George and came out of the Land Rover to look around: they looked up at some tall steel poles, that were used to transmit telegram and radio signals overseas, before returning to a lower level of the hospital grounds. Violet wanted to see the old maternity hospital which the Government had turned into a nursing home for indigents who could not afford the cost of one like the one in which mother's father spent his last days on earth. Then they visited that old nursing home which had been sold to a physician who was then conducting his own private nursing home for the elites in Tobago. Paul explained to the receptionist the reason for their visit, and they were allowed the visit the room where his father used to be.

On their way home Mr. Stanley Willis brought a subject which Paul and his son's mother seemed to be avoiding: "Ah wha mek yuh tink twa papal nar talk tuh wone ader? He asked. After pausing and getting no reply, he continued, "Eas fur eas meh car cee; eis wone ting dat culd beh raspansibal. Dat eis prid, an prud paple wuld neber entar deh Lard's kingdam. Misa Paul Scott, yuh an Maz Sharma Thamas fal eout meny yares aguh; ahyuh nuh tink dat eis tim fuh ahyuh fuh mek eup? Aul ahyuh ah duh, eis hurtin dis yangman whe ah knaw eis langin fuh cee eh parent tak tuh wone anadar." There was silence for a while then Violet spoke up: "Yes, Uncle Paul," she asked, "why don't you and Auntie Sherma speak to each other?"

Paul replied, "Why don't you ask her? I have nothing against her."

Sherma said, "I have nothing against Paul."

Mr. Stanley Willis said, "Aul yuh cee wha meh binah sah; eit beh suh lang dat nadar ah dem rambar wha mak dey fal eout. Deh langer ahyuh sta fuh tak tuh wone anadar, deh hardah fuh alyuh fuh mak eup."

Paul dropped off Violet at the *great house* then Mr. Stanley Willis at a little house near the former *pay yard* where he used to sleep. He took his son and Sherma home last. When Phillip had come out of the vehicle and as Sherma was coming out:

She said, "Good night, Paul."

And, he said, "Sleep tight, Sherma."

CHAPTER ELEVEN

A Church Wedding/The Orr Family Reunion

ABOUT A YEAR BEFORE the events, the Orr family had formed a central committee to plan what they were going do. However, as the time drew nearer, they formed a larger committee to decide what functions the various personnel would perform. They decided who would be in charge of security; who would greet the attendees; who would be the ushers, cooks, store keepers, etc. They were going to provide special caps and badges for each person to wear according to their function. Family members had gone ahead and construct several structures where various functions would be carried out. Donna and Aunt Enid must give their final approval of every function. Very soon the grand weekend approached, and everything was ready.

It was a busy weekend and one that many people were looking forward to -- the people had a double reason to celebrate, and from early on Saturday afternoon a crowd began to assemble. One would introduce oneself: "Ah eis yuh cusin Desmand; yuh uncle Rupert beh maried tuh fuh meh auntie Truly" or "Yuh cusin Elpedia son, wha beh nam Dalmanie, an fuh meh fus cusin Filbert hah deh sam fadar"; or "Yuh grat grandfadar Knally did hah twa pickney wit fuh meh madar aunt yungar sistar, wha beh nam Josephine", etc. Tobago is a very small island and the people from the various villages are related; and if one were from Tobago, one was a member of the Orr family. Therefore, no invitation to the event was really necessary. However, no one came empty handed; but, everyone brought something to contribute to the occasion. People donated small animals; home grown chickens, wild meats, such as the tattoo (armadillo), agouti, and possum; ground provisions, rice, wheat f lour, sea moss punch, and alcoholic, as well as, non-alcoholic beverages, to name a few items.

Some men were beating bongo drums and tambourine, while others were playing in a tambu bamboo band. They had killed a cow and alcoholic, as well as, non-alcoholic beverages were consumed, as they ceremoniously cooked the cow's head. The stew was a broth of the cow's head, young bananas, small wheat f lour dumplings, very hot peppers and other ingredients. Eating that food was supposed to make a man feel very macho, and one was expected to drink the broth without shedding any tears. Anyone who felt sleepy during the night would look for a remote location to catch a wink; others didn't sleep at all that night, as they were planning to begin cooking early next day.

They had put up different tents that were framed with bamboo, and had thatched roofs made out of dry coconut branches; some of these tents were to be used as cooking stations and store rooms. Once a pot was cooked, the cooks brought the cooked food to a central storeroom of which Mr. Amman and Uncle Timothy were the store keepers. Miss Ellen was there with Violet Scott-Ramdeen; they had volunteered to help wait on the table in the big tent for the wedding party. Mrs. Sandra Scott, however, was more or less, just a spectator, and spent most of the time speaking to Suzanne and Charles who had come from America. The families had taken orders from each person of the wedding party and knew ahead of time what food each person wanted. The table was made in the shape of a horse shoe, and while the guests were being served, at various times some servers went around on the inside of the table with exotic items, and if a guest desired a specialty, the server would give it to him/her.

The church wedding was scheduled to take place at a Shouter Baptist church at 1 p.m., Sunday, and the officiating leader was the same person from San Fernando, Trinidad, who had exorcised the evil inf luence from the river by the bay many years ago. Vasthi a local seamstress had outfitted the ladies of the wedding party, after Donna had over-ruled her aunt Enid from Canada about having the dresses made in New York. Vasthi was a talented dressmaker who must have inherited her excellent sewing talent from her late father who was one of the best tailors in the area: she would cut several dresses at a time, and have her younger sister and a first cousin help her to hem and stitch them, or do anything that called for less skill. The males wore tuxedos that were rented from a newly opened men's store at a shopping mall in Scarborough. However, the groom, Mickey and his sons brought their own suits from America. Mickey also bought a suit for his brother, Selwyn, and another for Mr. Stanley Willis, which the latter accepted as if it were a gift from heaven. Upon leaving the church, the wedding party went on a motorcade to the Scarborough Botanic Garden to take pictures, after which they drove past the wedding reception venue on another ride towards Roxborough. While they had gone to the church, anyone at the reception venue who wanted to eat at the table under the big tent would be served. However, as the motorcade passed Belle Garden on the second motorcade, some women went to the big tent and said, "Everybodie, clare eout fram dis table, ahwee hah tuh lay eit fuh deh married people dem." Whereupon, they spread a white table cloth; brought out a beautiful wedding cake, which was placed at the head of the table; and laid China wares to serve the wedding party.

When the wedding party arrived, the parents of the bride and groom, Mr. Isaac and Mrs. Nellie Orr and Mr. Herbert and Judy Reid, respectively, were at the entrance of the big tent to greet them with a glass of wine from the bride's parents for the groom, and another from the groom's parents for the bride, before sitting them at the head of the table. Mickey had given his sister away, and he was the master of ceremony at the reception. While the guests were eating they were entertained by various spokesmen and women, singers, limbo, bongo, and moko jumbie dancers. The Belle Garden Steel Orchestra rendered some special musical selections, during which the Sherma, Paul and Phillip participated in playing various steel pan instruments. Although Mr. Stanley Willis was not on the agenda to participate at the official wedding reception ceremony, he was allowed to speak at a section that was opened to anyone who wished to give his/her admonitions/congratulations to the bride and groom: First he expressed his gratitude to "Misa Mickey Orr" for bringing him a lovely Yankee suit from America; then he said that the wedding was an answer to his prayers; he had been praying for a long time that the couple would get married: "Ah used tuh tel Miz Donna Orr dat shah hah fuh set ah good axample fuh sheh dartar dem. Meh glad dat shah farder finally geh Misa Kannath Raid fuh maried tuh sheh, an may God bles dem always inah dey mariage."

Mr. Ramdeem was at the reception with his daughter Rookmine and her husband, and he surprised everyone by playing on a borrowed bongo drum, before extending congratulations on behalf of his entire family. (He and his brothers used to play music in an East Indian music band a long time ago.) He also drew everyone's attention to the fact that it was he who had designed the wedding rings, and reminded them how the two families had been friends for a very long time ever since Mr. Timothy had sold him some gold; that Mickey was his son in law, and that he was very proud of Mickey and Phyllis' two sons. He added, "Hope ahyuh nuh forget dat ah ches ah gol stil missin inah theh riber or som whare; nuh badie seh dat theh fine am yet. Meh affarin tap dallars fuh am."

When they had come to a part of the proceedings at the wedding reception where the bride would throw her bouquet over her shoulder, while all the single women tried to see who would catch it, Mr. Stanley Willis shouted, "Whe Miz Shrama Thamas? Ahyuh wat til sheh com tuh cee eif sheh wuld cetch eam." However, Sherma would have none of it and refused the join the single women. He called upon Paul to stand with the single men as their turn came to see who would catch the bride garters after the groom had thrown it in a similar fashion. However, Paul had gone to sit in his vehicle and did not want to participate. After the bride and groom stuck the cake and kissed, they called upon one of the unmarried young couples to withdraw the knives from the cake; Selwyn and his partner got to do the honor.

When the ceremony was over they brought out wooden stilts of various heights, and limbo equipment, for anyone who dared to practice their skills at being a moko jumbie or limbo dancer; and it was much fun to see some old folks trying to relive their youths among the persons who attempted to show off their dancing skills. The crowd pitched in to clean up, as the wedding party was leaving, but some children and other young people carried on with impromptu games until about 11 p. m. The next day was Easter Monday and a crowd would be at Belle Garden beach to see an annual sailing boat race from Scarborough to Roxborough pass by. Members of the Orr family congregated on a portion of the beach near Grandie River. There were much food wastes from the wedding reception the day before, and Mickey and Phyllis were proud to see their two boys then helping Uncle Timothy and their uncle Selwyn to feed the pigs. Some visiting family members from abroad spread big bath towels and lay in the sand, soaking up the warm sunshine, as they waited to see the boats sail by; others built a bon fire and roasted breadfruits; while some made fire places out of big stones to cook rice and peas which they boiled down with coconut milk, small fish and other ingredients, added to the pot. When the race was in sight, most people rushed to Man of War Hill from where they could see the end of the race, and some boys took the opportunity to raid the food that was still cooking.

The next big events took place the following day: The Annual Goat and Crab Races in Tobago. These were held at Bucco on the western end of Tobago; and people would come from other islands to see those events. It was the last opportunity for all the family to see one another; as most of them would be unable to do so for a very long time. They took some pictures of themselves and friends posing together. Mr. Stanley Willis wore his new suit specifically because he wanted to pose with "Misa Mickey Orr" and his immediate family; and to take another picture with "Misa Kenneth Reid an Miz Dana Orr and der twu dartar." He said, "Ahwee mae nat cee wone anader ein parsan gain pan dis erth; bur, ah hop tuh cee yahal ein haban."

The Shouter Baptists from Trinidad had another opportunity to enjoy the hospitality of the Orr family. Most of them spent a week in Tobago after Easter. And, they would hold religious meeting almost nightly by the roadsides. Before the immediate family members that had come from abroad left, Mrs. Sandra Scott- Ramdeen hosted a banquet for them. The family members would leave Tobago on various dates, as the schedules of their departures were at different times. Aunt Enid and her two sons would return to Canada the Saturday after Easter, Therefore, Sandra held the banquet that Friday night before. Paul had invited son, who in turn invited his mother. Sherma had not been to the *great house* since a long time ago on the night she broke up with Paul, and everything seemed to be the same. After the dinner, while the children were performing songs and skits for the adults, Sherma and her son slipped away to beneath a big old silk cotton tree in the back of the *great house,* where Paul had tried to make her use illicit drugs, and as they were speaking Paul joined them. At first, she seemed to be speaking to Paul through Phillip; and Paul seemed to speaking to her through Phillip, too. But, before they rejoined the others inside, they would talk directly to each other.

Phillip had to leave the following Sunday because his time to go back to America was up. His mother had planned to travel back on the same plane with him, and his father Paul dropped them to Crown Point Airport. Phillip's cousin Violet and Mr. Stanley Willis went with them, and Mr. Stanley Willis was very pensive all along the way. While they were waiting for the travelers to check in, Paul tried to get into his head: he wanted to know about what he was thinking. At first, Mr. Stanley Willis wanted to know what they had thought of his speech at the wedding, and how he looked in the new suit Mr. Mickey had bought him; then, he looked at Phillip and said, "Meh culd hadly balief dat dis yang man mak sach ah nam fuh eiself: heh ah big enginaire." And, speaking to Paul and Sherma, he added, "heh mak deh twu ahyuh fel prud; bur, haw ahyuh mak em fel, tuh cee dat eih parant nuh maried. Lok haw Maz Danna Orr an Misa Kenneth Reid darters beh lok heppy tuh cee dair parent dem gat marrad."

Paul interrupted him. "What are you trying to say, Mr. Stanley Willis?"he asked.

Mr. Stanley Willis replied, "Maz Violat Ramdeen an Misa. Philip Scatt lasenin; bur, whah axample ahyuh shawin dem, fuh knuw dat ahyuh nuh marrad?"

Sherma said, "Le wee change the subject, please, Mr. Stanley Willis; p-l-e-a-s-.

It was a very touching parting scene to behold Violet and Phillip, who asked her to convey his best wishes to all his cousins in London when she go there. When Phillip and his mother were boarding their flight, Paul said, "Call me when you reach home."

And, Sherma replied, "You bet; we will."

The other family members who had come from America had more time to spend in Tobago. Mrs. Sandra Scott-Ramdeen had invited Suzanne and Charles to spend a couple of days with them at the *great house* after Easter Tuesday. There were many places of interest Paul wanted to show Suzanne and Charles, and Mrs. Sandra and Violet adored their little girls; they showed them almost every inch of the *great house*. Charles was interested in making an investment in Tobago. He and Suzanne had talked about buying a piece of land and build a house there before the cost of land went beyond their reach. Also, he'd been encouraging his uncle the civil engineer to do the same. After all, his uncle had been always talking about an early retirement. *And, where was the best place to retire to, but Tobago? h*e had thought. Therefore, while Charles and Suzanne went with Paul to look at some properties, Phyllis took their two daughters with her for lunch at Rookmine's. Charles and Suzanne wanted to see if they could afford a down payment on any of the real estates that were up for sale; Paul was going to introduce them to some of his friends, and if they saw any property they liked, when they got back to America, they could wire the money back to Mina (Phyllis' sister) to acquire it for them.

Kenneth and Donna spent much of the remaining time with Selwyn, his mother and Uncle Timothy at the shop, when they were not tending the pigs. Several old friends would stop by to offer them congratulation on their marriage. Their two daughters visited many old friends from their former high school. Mickey visited his old primary school with his sons; and, a caretaker let them in: he wanted to show his boys where his old class room was. Things had changed: they now had computers on all the desks; but, he tried to recreate how it used to be. The two old cupboards were still there, and shoved before a column at the side of the class room; they were locked, and he wondered what were inside them. School was out on vacation, and no one was there to show him the inside. When it was time to go back to America, they all had planned to travel as a group, and when they were high in the sky, Suzanne and Charles' younger girl said to Kenneth and Donna's older daughter, "My name is Denise Donahue, what's yours?"

The other girl replied, "Mary Reid."

The little girl responded, "No; it's Mary Orr!"

Now, when she was born, she was registered as "Mary Orr"-- taking her mother's maiden name; but, now that her parents were married, and the family had an opportunity to change her last name when she had gotten her visa to come to America, she had adapted her father's last name.

The little girl went on, "You're lying; Mr. Stanley Willis said that if you didn't look someone in the eye when you're speaking to them, you're lying."

Mickey and Phyllis' sons were peering out the windows of the plane at the clouds, and the clouds seemed to be making various images in the sky: the boys could see what looked like Uncle Timothy and Selwyn feeding the pigs at Grandie River. They saw others that looked like their grandparents. Then, they saw one set of clouds floating toward them looking like a flock of sheep with someone like Mr. Stanley Willis in his new suit behind them, and they remembered what he had told them: "Ef yuh want papal tuh raspect yuh, leh dem cal yuh buh yuh ful name, an lok yuh ina yuh eyes."

KEY

(Note that some chapters are not listed because there
were no local dialects in those chapters)

PREFACE

a) Ah finish shoppin' oui.
    I've completed my shopping, you know?

b) Yuh get al yuh want?
    Have you gotten all you wanted?

c) She said, "Thank yuh; well, ah had tuh duh, wha' ah ha tuh duh.
    She said, "Thank you; Well, I had to do, what I had to do.

CHAPTER 1

a) Ah who ya alredy tell bout al dis?
    To whom have you already told about all this?

b) Weh rich!
    We're rich!

c) Ahwee hav tuh protec dese treasurs fore deh government tek dem way
    fram ahwee
    *We have to protect these treasures before the government takes them away
    from us*

d) The Buccaneers woul kill wone ah deh pirates an leave em tuh guard
    any treasur dey bin ah leave behind.

The Buccaneers would kill one of their pirates and leave him to guard any treasures they would leave behind.

e) Meh believeh dat deh dead pirate guardin deh treasur be angry dat yuh mov dem
   I believe that the dead pirate guarding the treasure is angry that you moved them

f) Maybe, deh bawye right; ena al mi forty-five years meh neber cee rain lik dis
   Maybe, the boy's right; in all my forty-five years I've never seen rain like this

g) Ah wonda how much damag dis rain alredy caused; howeber, ahwee ha tuh wait til dis bad weatha ober, fuh weh tuh fine out
   I wonder how much damage this rain already caused; however, we have to wait until this bad weather's over, to find out

h) Maybeh, Dad and Uncle Timothy geh catch up inah deh riber and beh wash out tuh sea
   Maybe, Dad and Uncle Timothy got caught up in the river and are washed out to sea

i) Ahwee beh think dat deh riber beh haul ahyoh way
   We had thought that the river had taken you away

j) Eh didn't; bur eh seam as duh ahwee lost deh ches ah gold
   It didn't; but, it seemed as though we've lost the chests of gold

k) Whe was the watchman?
   Where was the watchman?

l) Ah ha nuh job, nuh money; Mr. Peter Scott, whil yuh waitin fuh yuh insurance money, ina deh meantim, wha yuh want meh and meh family fuh duh?

I have no job, no money; Mr. Peter Scott, while you're waiting for your insurance money, in the meantime, what you want me and my family to do?

CHAPTER 2

a) Ahyuh fine wone ah dem! Ahwee hav tuh guh and get eit, fore someone beat ahwee tuh eit
   You found one of hem! We have to go and get it, before someone beat us to it

b) Here yuh eis
   Here you are

c) Ah would guh tuh Trinidad wit Ossie an bring alang ah sample ah deh gol tuh show tuh sume ah dem East Indian jewelers, and cee how much dey guh pay meh fuh eit
   I would go to Trinidad with Ossie and bring along a sample of the gold to show to some of those East Indian jewelers to see how much they would pay me for it

d) Al yuh duh, nuh leh dem try tuh get am fram yuh fuh nothing; yuh hav tuh haggle wit dem fuh com eup wit ah good bargen.
   All you do, don't let them try to get it from you for nothing; you have to haggle with them to come up with a good bargain

e) Misa Ramdeen!
   Mr. Ramdeen!

f) Timothy! Wha ina deh world bring yuh tuh Arima?
   Timothy! What in the world brought you to Arima?

g) Wi want yuh tuh put ahwee eon tuh ah honest jewelry-dealah. Ahwee hav som gol fuh sale
   We want you to put us on to an honest jewelry-dealer. We have some gold for sale

h) Yuh com tuh deh right place. Ah doz mek meh own jewelry; ah ha meh own assay department whe meh nephew workin; an weh doesn't rab anybody. Weh hav ah good reputation round yah

You came to the right place. I make my own jewelry; I have my own assay-department, where my nephew is working, and we don't rob anyone. We have a good reputation around here

i) Right away ah can tel dat dis eis good stuff. How muh eof dis duh yuh hav?

Right away I could tell that this is good stuff; how much do you have?

j) Wi hav ah ches lik dat wone full

We have a chest like that one full

k) Ah guh pay $2,000. 00 dollars fuh dem. Eif al ah dem eis jus lik deh wone yuh want tuh sell meh, and ah doe eben hah tuh assay dem befor ah buy dem, dis eis really good stuff

I will pay you $ 2,000.00 dollars for them. If all of them is just like the one that want to sell me, and I don't even have to assay them before I buy them; this is really good stuff.

l) Leh wi shop around tuh cee eif wi culd get ah bettar deal

Let us shop around to see if we could get a better deal

m) Dem ader dealars guh rab yuh, dey wuld charge yuh al sort ah fees. Ah hate tuh cee yuh fellars get rab. Ah guh giv yuh $2,100.00 dallars -- take it or leav eit. Dat eis meh final affah

These other dealers will rob you, they would charge all sort of fees. I hate to see you fellows get rob. I'll give you $2,100.00 -- take it or leave it. That's my final offer.

n) Everybody rond here goin tuh ask yuh how much ah did affa yuh, befor givin yuh ah price; dey know dat ah set deh standards and dat ah eis deh best deala round; ah bet dat yuh won't get ah betta deal

Everybody around here are going to ask you how much I did offer you, before giving you a price; they know that I set the standards and that I am the best dealer around; I bet that you won't get a better deal

o) Now, yuh fellas will hav tuh mak up yuh mind. Bring deh rest euf deh stuff tuh meh and yuh don't hav tuh wait fuh ah single day tuh get yuh money
   Now, you fellows will have to make up your minds. Bring the rest of the stuff to me and you don't have to wait for a single day to get your money

p) Wha eif yuh set ahwee up, an ha som euf yuh bways amdush wi? Deposit deh money ina ah bank unda his nam, an yuh car meet ahwee ein Scarborough at deh port whe ahwee guh deliver deh gol tuh yuh. Wi guh giv yuh ah receipt statin dat yuh buy deh stuff fram ahwee. Yuh car bring alang witness tuh say dat wee deliver deh items tuh yuh
   What if you set us up and have some of your boys ambush us? Deposit the money in a bank under his name, and you can meet us in Scarborough at the port where we'll deliver the gold to you. We'll give you a receipt stating that you bought the stuff from us. You can bring along witnesses to say that we deliver the items to you

q) Dat's nat how weh duh business; eif yuh fellas nat serious, duh waste meh time. Yuh war tuh mak ah deal or nat?
   That's not how we do business; if you fellows not serious, don't waste my time. You want to make a deal or not?

r) Meh alda broder Isaac ha deh final say ina dis matta
   My older brother Isaac has the final say in this matter

s) Ok, ah guh meet yuh fellars en Scarborough. Wha yuh think bout next Tuesday?
   Ok, I'll meet you fellers in Scarborough. What you think about next Tuesday?

t) Dat should't beh ah problem
    That shouldn't be a problem

u) Ah guh giv yuh $200.00 eas ah depasit an yuh culd leav deh wone
    yuh hav wit meh
    I'll give you $200.00 as a deposit and you could leave the one you have
    with me

v) Tak eit
    Take it

w) Ef yuh fellas ha anymo gold fuh geh rid eof, remember meh
    If you fellers have anymore gold to get rid of remember me

CHAPTER 4

a) Paul Scott, ah hear yuh as comin back tuh Tobago; yuh most grow
    up tuh beh ah big man, ber yuh wuldn't giv up yuh boyhood pranks.
    Ah member how yuh lov tuh hang eout wit meh; ber, ah busy now.
    When ah ha tim, ahwee guh si down and tark, and yuh guh tel meh
    all bout Landan
    Paul Scott, I heard that you were coming back to Tobago; you have almost
    grown to be a big man, but you wouldn't give up your boyhood pranks.
    I can remember how you loved to hang out with me; but, I'm busy now.
    When I have time, we' ll sit down and talk and you' ll tell me all about
    London

b) Now, Paul Scott, ah knaw how yuh venturous; ber, doh yuh guh lokin
    fer noh treasure ina dese waters, cause plenty alligators hare
    Now, Paul Scott, I know how you're adventurous; but, don't you go looking
    for any treasures in these waters, because there're plenty of alligators here.

c) Dat ah lat ah figurin yuh hah tuh duh, Paul Scott; yuh knaw? Bur,
    meh believ dat yuh culd handle eit

That's a lot of figuring you'll have to do, Paul Scott; you know? But, I believe that you could handle it

d) Wi car m-e-e-t ah deh foud maket ah Scarbro dis comin weekend; som fellars fram Trinidad wuld bring tings tuh Tobago tuh sell. Dey might kno wha yuh lokin fah

We can meet at the food market at Scarborough this coming weekend, some fellows from Trinidad would bring things to Tobago to sell. They may know what you're looking for

e) Ah doh war yuh guh hangin eout wit dat bway enymo. Eif was yuh deh police hold wit drug, all dis tim yuh bin rottin ina jail --wane law fuh deh rich and wone fuh deh por. Forget bout deh gol wha missin, wone day som lucky parson guh fine eit. Eim deh meantime, just tink bout yuh futha

I don't want you to hang out with that boy anymore. If 'twas you the police held with drugs, all this time you would've been rotting in jail -- one law for the rich and one for the poor. Forget about the gold that's missing; one day some lucky person will find it. In the meantime, just think about your future

f) Paul Scott, ah knows dat yuh eis yung; ber, yuh ha yuh whol futha head eof yuh. Settle down and mek someting eof yuhself. Yuh tel meh dat yuh culd kep bok and yuh plan tuh tek ober deh offic fram deh gal ah deh pay-yard, an dat yuh an meh guh run deh estate. Eif dis eis deh way yuh plan tuh cary eon, betah yuh fadar sen yuh back ah Englan fuh beh wit yuh madar

Paul Scott, I know that you're young; but, you have your whole future ahead of you. Settle down and make something of yourself. You told me that you could keep book and you plan to take over the office from the girl at the pay-yard and that you and me will run the estate. If this is the way you plan to carry on, it would be better that your father send you back to England to with your mother

g) Doe embarrass yuh fadar; yuh father culd mak arrangement fuh deh vehicle licen inspectar fuh com arn giv yuh ah drivin tes rite pan dis estate and wen yuh hah deh licen, yuh an meh culd duh deh shappin pan weekend, an leh yuh por fader rest up

Don't embarrass your father; your father could make arrangements for the vehicle inspector to come and give you a driving test right on this estate, and when you have the license, you and me could do the shopping on weekend, and let your poor father rest up

h) Sumtime meh, tuh, culd com lang fuh deh ride arn tuh lif anyting dat tuh havy fuh aryah tuh cary. Paul, yuh cud hah ah brite futha. Eit hah adar Wite bways yuh age down ah low side dat yuh culd associat wit arn leav dis drug buisnes lon

Sometimes I, too, could come along for the ride to lift anything that's too heavy for you to carry. Paul, you could have a bright future. It has other White boys your age down at low side that you could associate with and leave this drug business alone

i) Paul Scott, yuh tel meh dat yuh culd kep bok; at fus, meh nuh beh believ yuh. Bur, tuh cee eis tuh beliv: Meh neber hare yuh fadar, nar Misa Kenneth Brown, nar deh bok-keper, sah yuh mak ah mistak yet. Yuh doin fine pan am, Paul Scott.

Paul Scott, you told me that you could keep book; at first, I didn't believe you. But, to see is to believe: I've never heard your father, nor Mr. Kenneth Brown, nor the book-keeper, say that you made a mistake as yet. You're doing fine at it, Paul Scott.

CHAPTER 5

a) Can yuh spar meh ah qartar?
Could you spare me a quarter?

b) Doe giv eim. Des bways duh nothin, ber use drugs an harass people a-l-l day lang

Don't give him. These boys do nothing, but harass people all day long

c) Didn't ah cee yuh installin ah pane ah glas buh wa jewelry stor en Tobago yestaday?
Didn't I see you installing a pane of glass by a jewelry store in Tobago yesterday?

d) Yuh sure did, eis ah lucky ting ah didn't commit ah crime, an yuh wasn't deh polic lokin fuh meh
You sure did; it's a lucky thing that I didn't commit a crime, and that you weren't the police looking for me.

e) Ah jus gat aff deh plen rite dis minute, an tek ah taxi ina town; ah livin jus ah deh tap eof dis hill
I just got off the plane right this minute, and took a taxi into town; I'm living just at the top of this hill

f) Wher yuh knoh meh fram? Are yuh fram Trinidad?
Where do you know me from? Are you from Trinidad?

g) Ah fram Tobago: bur, ah used tuh cee yuh an meh fus cusin husban ein deh newspaper al deh time eas yuh enta various bady buildin exhibition
I'm from Tobago; but, I used to see you and my first cousin's husband in the newspapers all the time as you enter various body building exhibitions

h) An yuh mak meh out fram only deh pictures? Eit es ah smal world dat weh livin ein
And you made me out from only the pictures? It's a small world that we're living in

i) Ah cee yuh eis ah man eof gold
I see that you're a man of gold

j) People always admiah meh rings; yuh kno? Ramdeen fram Arima mek dese. Meh sistar liv nat tuh far way fram heh stor ein Arima, an ebery tim ah guh tuh cee sheh, man, ah must pas ina Ramdeem. Deh man eis competin gainst dem big stor lik Y deh Menis an heh holdin heh own. Al heh children dem was ein deh business; bur, now som ah dem ein school ein Englan, aders ein America, eor ein Caneda. Wha eis yuh fus cusin husband nam?

People always admire my rings; you know? Ramdeen from Arima made these. My sister lives not far away from his store in Arima, and every time I go to see her, man, I must pass in Ramdeen's. The man is competing against those big stores like Y de Menis and he's holding his own. All his children were in the business; but, now some of them are in school in England, others in America, or in Canada. What's your first cousin's husband's name?

k) Bway, Albert eis meh g-o-o-d pander; heh an meh used tuh wok out ina ah gym ein Belmont, Port eof Spain ein deh evenin

Boy, Albert's my good partner; he and I used to work out in a gym in Belmont, Port of Spain in the evening

l) Wone eof meh uncle fren beh tak meh an meh fren Johnny tuh Ramdeen befor. Ein fac, meh fadar an meh uncle sel em som gol. Dem Caribs stil livin ina dey vilege ein Arima? Deh same uncle fren beh tak weh tuh cee how dey livin: eis jus eas weh beh read ina weh readin bok ah schol

One of my uncle's friends had taken my friend Johnny and me to Ramdeen's before. In fact, my father and uncle sold him some gold. Are those Caribs still living in their village in Arima? The same uncle's friend had taken us to see how they were living: it was just as we had read in our reading books at school

m) Dere nuh riber eon Richmond Street

There's no river on Richmond Street

n) Ded yuh kno dat eis cause yuh blond wha mak meh maried yuh?
Did you know that it's because you're blonde why I married you?

o) Miz, doe shoot. Ah ain't trublin yuh; ah jus gat aff wok an mar hury fuh gat hom,; ah hah tuh gat eup early ein deh marnin
Miss, don't shoot. I'm not troubling you; I just got off work and I'm hurrying to get home; I have to get up early in the morning

CHAPTER 6

a) Finally, eit seem eas thugh yuh inten tuh settle dung, an gih yuh parant sam gra- picknay
Finally, it seems as though you intend to settle down, and give your parents some grandchildren

b) Nuh mek heh gat way fram yuh; nuh? Yuh knah haw lang meh bin ah sen an tel dat bway fuh maried tuh wone ah dem Yankee waman, an gih heh fedar sam Yankee gra- picknay?
Don't make him get away from you; No? You knew how long I've been sending and telling that boy to marry to one of those Yankee women, and give his father some Yankee grandchildren?

CHAPTER 9

a) Misa Mickey Orr, yuh doe knah haw mach yuh mak meh feel prud?
Mr. Mickey Orr, you don't know how much you've made me feel proud?

b) Whah yuh larfin ath? Dat eis yuh nam; yuh knoh? Eif yuh war pepel fuh respec yuh, yuh hah fuh leh dem cal yuh buh yuh ful nam, an lok yuh ina yuh eye
What are you laughing at? That's your name; you know? If you want people to respect you, you have to let them call you by your full name, and look at you in your eyes

c) Meh nuh hah enby inah meh hart fuh nuh badie; bur' eif nuh binah fuh yuh, nun eof dese tings wuldah tak plac. Eis yuh wheh fus fin deh gol; an yuh fedar an yuh uncle brin dem tuh Engin Town meny yares ahgo. An, wen rain beh wash eit way, ah suh meh gat tuh fine deh fus ches eof gol; an Misa Ramdeen gat fuh fine deh secand wone. Ah suh dem cume heh dem richas. Deh Scotts and deh Ramdeens duin wel; an, meh glad tuh seh dat deh nuh lef yuh eout. Meh ole an meh nuh beh tek bok, suh meh nuh beh expec mach. Meh hah wone pickney and sheh nuh beh lik school, tuh. Sheh hardly culd cumb sheh hare whan sheh hah sheh fus pickney

I don't have envy in my heart for anyone; but, if it weren't for you, none of these things would've taken place. It's you who first find the gold; and your father and uncle brought them to Engine Town many years ago. And, when rain washed them away, it's so I found the first chest of gold; and, Mr. Ramdeen found the second one. That's how they came by their riches. The Scotts and the Ramdeens doing well; and I'm glad to see that they didn't leave you out. I'm old and I didn't take book, so I wasn't expecting much. I have one child and she didn't like school, too. She could hardly comb her hair when she had her first child

d) Haw eis yuh cusin, Miz Suzanne Thamas, dat jain yuh ina America doin?

How's your cousin, Miss Suzanne Thamas, who joined you in America is doing?

e) Yuh madar sistar packney ah war poiceman ina Caneda? Meh L-o-r-d; whan yuh hah ambishan yuh culd beh anyting dat yuh want tuh beh.

Your mother's sister's child's a policeman in Canada? My L-o-r-d; when you have ambition, you could be anything that you want to be

f) Yuh family shuld hah ah reunian, tuh; Suh dat, dem whea nuh hah nah ambishan, woulda beh farce tuh lok eup. Ah mean dat dey wuld becam mativated. Discus eit wit yuh fadar an yuh mada befo yuh guh bac toh Ameraca. Wrate yuh antie ina Caneda an aryuh plan somting eas soon eas passible. Eit doe hav tuh bah dis yare; ber, deh soonah deh bettah

Your family should have a reunion, too. So that, those who don't have any ambition, would be forced to look up. I mean that they would become motivated. Discuss it with your father and mother before you go back to America. Write your auntie in Canada and you all plan something as soon as possible. It doesn't have to be this year; but, the sooner the better

CHAPTER 10

a) Meh nuh war tuh guh truwh dat agan; eif deyh gol shaw eup, whosaeber fin eam guh beh deh lacky wone

I don't want to go through that again; if the gold shows up, whosoever finds it would be the lucky one

b) Ah wah mak yuh tink two papal nar tark tuh wone andar? He asked; eas fur eas meh car cee, eis wne ting dat culd beh raspansibal: dat eis prid; an prud papal wuld nebar anfar deh Lard's Kindam. Misa Paul Scatt an Maz Sheama Philip yuh fal eout many yares agaw; Ahyuh nuh tink dat eis tim fuh ahyuh fuh mek eup? Aul ahyuh ah duh eis hurtin dis yangman, whe ah eis langin fuh cee eh parant tark tuh wone anadar

Why do you think that two people won't speak to each other? As far as I can see, it's only one thing that could be responsible: that's pride. And, proud people would never enter the Lord's kingdom. Mr. Paul Scott and Miss Sherma Phillp, you fell out many years ago, don't you think that it's time to make up? All you are doing is hurting this young man, who's longing to see his parents talk to each other.

c) Ahyuh cee whe meh binah sah; eit ah bin sah lang, dat nadar ah dem membar wah mak dey fal eout. Deh langar ahyuh sta fuh tark tuh wone anadar, deh hardar fuh aryuh fuh mak eup

You see what I was saying; it has been so long, that neither of them remembers what made them fall out. The longer you stay to talk to one another, the harder 'twill be for you to make up

CHAPTER 11

a) Ah eis yuh cusin Desmand: yuh uncle Rupart beh maried tuh fuh meh auntie Truly; or, Yuh cusin Elpheda son, whe be name Dalmanie, an fuh meh fus cusin Filbut hah deh same fardar; or Yuh grat granfardar Knally did hah twa pickney wit fuh meh madar antie yangar sistar, wha beh nam Josephine

I'm your cousin Desmond: Your uncle Rupert was married to my auntie Truly; or, Your cousin Elpheda's son named Dalmonie and my first cousin Filbert, had the same father; or, Your great grandfather Knolly had two children with my mother's aunt's younger sister named Josephine

b) Everybadie clare eout fram dis table; ahwee hah tuh lay eit fuh deh maried people dem

Everybody, clear out from this table; we have to lay it for the married people

c) Ah used tuh tel Miz Donna Orr dat sheh hah fuh set ah good axample fuh sheh dartar dem. Meh glad dat sheh fardar finally gat Misa Kenneth Reid fuh marred tuh sheh, an may God always bles dem inah dey marage

I used to tell Miss Donna Orr that she had to set good example for her daughters. I'm glad that her father finally got Mr. Kenneth Reid to marry her, and may God always bless them in their marriage

d) Hope ahyuh nuh forgat dat ah ches ah gol stil missin inah theh riber or som whare; nuh badie sheh dat theh fine am yet. Meh affarin tap dollars fuh am

Hope you all don't forget that a chest of gold is still missing in the river or some where; nobody said that that they found it as yet. I'm offering top dollars for it

e) Whe Miz Shama Thamas? Ahyuh wait til sheh com, tuh cee eif sheh wuld catch eam

Where's Miss Sherma Thomas? You a ll wait until she comes, to see if she would catch it

f) Ahwee mae nat cee wone anadar ein parsan gain pan dis eath; bur, ah hop tuh cee yahal ein heban
We may not see one another in person again upon this earth; but, I hope to see you all in heaven

g) Meh culd hardly belief dat dis yang man mak such ah nam fuh eiself: heh ah big enginaire
I could hardly believe that this young man has made a name for himself: he's a big engineer

h) Heh mak deh twa aryuh fel prud; ber, haw alyuh makin em fel, tuh cee dat eih parant dem nuh marad?
He made the two of you feel proud; but, how are you making him feel, to see they his parents aren't married?

i) Lok how Miz Danna Orr and Misa Kenneth Reid darter dem beh lok happy tuh cee dair parat dem get marad
Look how Miss Donna Orr and Mr. Kenneth Reid's daughters did look happy to see their parents get maried

j) Miz Violet Ramdeen an Misa Philip Scatt lisenin; ber, wah axample ahyuh shawin dem fuh knaw dat aryuh nuh marrad?
Miss Violet Ramdeen and Mr. Phillip Scott are listening; but, what example are you showing them, to know that you aren't married?

k) Le wee change deh subject, please
Let's change the subject, please

l) Eif yuh war papal tuh raspec yuh, leh dem cal yuh buh yuh ful nam, an lok yuh ina yuh eye
If you want people to respect you, let them call you by your full name, and look you in your eyes